I0733792

JILL BOYCE

# Royally Blessed

By

## Jill Boyce

ISBN-13: 978-1-959788-60-7

# Dedication

For my children, Isaac and Isabel, who bring laughter
and joy into my life and make this mother's heart proud.

# ACKNOWLEDGMENTS

I praise God, who whispered these stories to my heart and placed the perfect people along my writing path at the perfect time.

I thank my husband, children, family, and friends for their love and support.

I am grateful to Sherri Stewart, my editor for this book, who made the story shine and encouraged me along the way.

I'm appreciative to my publisher, Cynthia Hickey, for believing in my work.

I especially thank my mother, who passed away six years ago on the day of my daughter's birth. Her death inspired my first book, *Harte Broken*. She instilled in me the love of books and the desire to dream big. I love you, Mom.

My hope is my stories will provide comfort, laughter, and encouragement to my readers. May God bless you all.

"Have I not commanded you? Be strong and courageous. Do not be afraid; do not be discouraged, for the Lord your God will be with you wherever you go." Joshua 1:9 (NIV)

# Chapter 1

**Claire's hand shook** as she patted a damp washcloth across her forehead. Waking up before the sun had a chance to arise to meet her grandmother had brought on some dizziness. "What did you say?" Her eyes darted toward the queen mother's face, searching for some small bit of encouragement.

Her royal grandmother didn't usually exhibit much emotion, but today she'd become unmasked—at least for her. The queen mother straightened her posture from her chair planted directly across from Claire. She'd called her granddaughter, the current ruling queen of Amorley, to meet her for breakfast, and it looked like she had important matters to discuss.

Her grandmother removed her glasses, letting them hang around her neck from a gilded chain, and frowned. "I asked if you intended to give me a stroke and an untimely death."

Her heart sank—she hated disappointing her

grandmother. Claire had been coronated many months ago and had ruled the country well since then. Still, she had jumped from her warm and safe bed as soon as her grandmother beckoned. Old habits and all.

In the months since Albert's passing, the fire, her wedding, her unplanned pregnancy, and the very unplanned announcement of said pregnancy by the boisterous Margaret Thomson, her American granny, Claire had probably set a record for most scandals in a given time period. "I'm sorry, Grandmother. I feel terrible about the way the news became public. I certainly didn't intend to vomit onstage and didn't plan to share my pregnancy news with the world like that—especially not so soon. It just sort of…came out…literally."

"Harrumph," the queen mother grunted. "Well, I should think not. I don't have to tell you what an embarrassment it was for the world to find out this way."

Claire slumped in her seat, nausea coursing through her. She didn't know if its source came from the baby or the weight of expectation on her shoulders from the first months as Amorley's ruler, but her skin grew clammy again. Claire loved Ethan and knew she would love her baby. Still, doubt circled her mind about her capability to balance family life with running a country—not to mention tending to her responsibilities at the hospital. What if she failed? What if she let everyone down? What if she let herself down? She patted the washcloth across her neck to no avail. "I know. I'm so, so sorry. What do we do now?"

The queen mother shook her head. "I don't know. That's why I hired a medical consultant for you. They will guide us along this path and ensure you have everything you need to stay healthy. I've also called Glenda Halstaff—" She let her words linger as if this tidbit of information required no further explanation and settled all of their problems.

Claire scrunched her forehead. "Who's Glenda Halstaff?"

The queen mother gasped. "Who's Glenda Halstaff? How can you ask such a thing? Have you buried your head in the ground since you arrived at the castle?"

*Apparently so.*

"Fraulein Halstaff is the premier authority on all things celebrity, etiquette, style, and manners—second only to Mademoiselle Couture. I requested Couture's help, but she couldn't come. Besides, Fraulein Halstaff heralds from Maltenstein. After the way things ended at your wedding with Hans, Lord Chicanery, and Maurelle trying to overthrow you, the Maltenstein king reached out to me. He wants to make amends and discuss a renewed alliance with Amorley." The queen mother raised her glasses, inspected an invisible smudge on them, and placed them on the bridge of her nose.

Claire frowned. "How can we possibly trust any of them?"

The queen mother pursed her lips and returned her attention to her granddaughter. "Perhaps we cannot, but at some point, striving for peace is in Amorley's best interest. The Maltenstein embassy is sending an entourage with Fraulein Halstaff that will precede the arrival of the king, His Royal Highness Franz Spickletz. Fraulein Halstaff will guide us through a proper formal pregnancy announcement. She will prepare you for public appearances over the coming months." The queen mother pursed her lips, appearing to be in deep thought.

Claire had a bad feeling. She'd seen that look before. It usually meant the following words out of her grandmother's mouth would land Claire wrapped in tulle like a mummy at some fancy park. "Is there more?"

"It's just... there's something else I haven't mentioned because I wanted to ensure that the rule still stood."

Claire's stomach clenched. "What is it?"

The queen mother pressed her lips into a thin line before responding, "The reason it's crucial we formally present your pregnancy to the world and demonstrate you as a picture of health is because...."

Frowning, Claire chewed her fingernail, something her grandmother hated for her to do. "Because what?" *What horrible requirement could there be left in the Amorley Constitution?*

"Because you must present an heir or the promise

of an heir by the anniversary of your coronation."

Claire's jaw dropped. "You can't be serious. How can the country dictate my due date? Who does that? It's unreasonable. It's archaic. It's barbaric."

"Yes, dear, I agree with you about all of that, but be that as it may, the fact remains that as it stands currently, the Amorley Constitution requires it. Fortunately, you are indeed pregnant. So that part is taken care of, but I don't want to put any doubt in the public's mind about the health of their queen or the country's future heir."

"We have to change that offensive rule. If not for me, then change it for future generations."

With a raised brow, the queen mother lifted a bell from the table between them. "May I?"

Claire suppressed the desire to roll her eyes. "Of course, though, I don't know how you can drink tea at a time like this."

The queen mother rang the bell, and the new head of the household, Nigel Wittendour, appeared in the doorway.

No one could ever replace Albert, Claire's former head of the household, who'd passed away in the fire at the castle. However, each week she'd worked with Nigel, she grew fonder and fonder of him.

The gentleman had salt and pepper hair and stood at least six feet tall. He wore the traditional attire as Albert had done and flashed the royal women a kind smile that caused weathered lines to crinkle around his eyes. Claire guessed he was close to Granny's age or maybe a few years younger.

"Yes, ma'am, how may I be of service?" he asked.

The queen mother settled her glasses on the bridge of her nose again. "Nigel, we would love some tea, please."

"Of course." He gave a slight bow and turned to fetch their refreshment. Minutes later, Nigel reappeared with a silver platter filled with teacups, saucers, and a kettle. He delivered the items to their table and tilted his head. "May I?"

Claire sent him a warm smile. "Yes, please. Thank you so much."

"It's my pleasure, Your Majesty." He filled both cups with the sweet-smelling hot beverage and straightened his posture. "Is there anything else I can do for you?"

Claire muffled under her breath, "Turn back time? That way, I wouldn't have embarrassed myself by upchucking the contents of my stomach in front of Parliament. I'd also take some help planning the perfect Fruhling Gala."

"Unfortunately, ma'am, I don't have a time machine. However, by my observation, you have carried yourself with great strength and poise thus far, and I am certain you can handle the Fruhling Gala. Anything else?" Nigel raised a brow.

She hadn't intended for him to hear her private rant. Claire's face warmed. "No, thank you."

He turned to leave and had almost exited the room when a whirlwind of red velour bowled into him. "Oof." He quickly righted himself and rose, extending his hand to the victim.

A ring-covered hand reached upward and allowed the freshly minted butler to assist her to a standing position. Once upright, Claire's granny, Margaret Thomson, brushed off bits of dust from her tracksuit and glared. "Young man, you'd better watch where you're going. You could have flattened me right out."

Nigel's face reddened. "My deepest apologies, ma'am. Are you hurt?"

Granny waved away his concern. "Of course not. I'm old, and these bones don't bounce as they used to, but I'm tougher than I look." She marched toward her granddaughter.

Nigel bowed, still flushed with embarrassment, and then left the room.

Claire shook her head. "Granny, you have to be more careful."

"I don't have time for careful. Neither do you." She huffed between breaths.

Claire pulled over another tufted wingback chair and placed it next to hers. She gestured for her granny to take a seat. "Breathe. Take a minute. You'll give yourself a heart attack if you aren't careful."

"I'm fine. I've already had my heart episode for this decade, and I'm not returning to a hospital anytime soon. I know you love that place, but I sure don't. No

sir, if I never see the inside of that building again, I'd—
"

"Granny. What happened? Focus," Claire interrupted her granny's rant.

"Right, right." She held a finger in the air to indicate that she needed a minute and hunched forward, placing her hands on her knees. After taking several slow, deep breaths, Granny sat up again. Leaning back in the chair, she closed her eyes for a second, which seemed like an eternity to Claire. When she opened them again, the color had drained from her face.

Claire frowned. "You look like you've seen a ghost. What is going on?"

Claire's other grandmother, the queen mother, had become accustomed to Granny's theatrics by now. Still, she pursed her lips.

Granny ignored the queen mother's disapproving expression. "Almost. What would you say if I told you Maurelle has escaped that high security, fancy prison and cannot be found? Anywhere. Poof. Gone." She gestured with her hand as if something had disappeared from her grasp.

Frowning, the queen mother lifted her teacup to her lips and took a sip. "I don't see how that's possible. No one has informed me of any of this."

*Could it be true?* Claire's heart pounded harder. She couldn't have heard her granny correctly. The last time she'd spoken to her stepmother, Queen Maurelle, she'd been on her way to prison for treason. "Escaped?

Maurelle? How? When?"

Granny shrugged. "I was reading my morning paper when the phone rang, and one of those highfalutin men dressed in a black suit and serious expression—you know, the ones that are supposed to keep you safe?"

Claire raised a brow. "My security detail?"

Granny snapped her fingers. "That's it. Well, one of those guys—the tall one who never smiles—received this phone call and grew all hush-hush, but you know me and my eagle-like hearing—"

Claire muttered, "More like spy-level nosiness."

Granny whipped her head toward her granddaughter. "What was that?"

Claire smiled. "Nothing. Continue."

Granny sent her a side-eyed glance. "Anyway, he became all quiet and whispery, and he didn't think I could hear him, but I heard him say that Maurelle Evercliff had escaped from prison. This morning. Today. I think he's on the way to tell you, or maybe they'll send one of those fixer-people like in my daytime crime shows." She waved a dismissive hand. "But either way, she's out—that crazy woman did it. I'm not surprised. If anyone could do it, it'd be her. She probably had accomplices or sympathizers on the inside. Who knows? Either way, she's out, and that can't be good news for you or any of us."

"So, what you're saying is—the woman who locked me in a secret room and left me for dead, who planned a coup to take over my country, who abandoned me in the Dark Forest—that woman is free again?"

Granny's tongue clicked—her version of an empathic confirmation. "Yes. Sure enough."

"She almost ruined Amorley's financial security and would have bled the country dry in exchange for Lord Chicanery's support. I wonder if the Maltenstein leadership knows about this." The room spun, and Claire leaned forward, tucking her head between her knees in an unladylike pose. It didn't matter, though. Maurelle was free. What would her stepmother do next? What could Claire do? Sit around and wait for her nemesis to come for her?

A hand settled on Claire's back and rubbed it gently. "There, there, honey. It'll be okay. If that woman tries anything, I'll take her down myself."

Turning her head to the side, Claire glanced at her granny.

Granny pumped her fist in the air like an athlete in a prize fight.

Claire sent Granny a slight grin. "I appreciate you wanting to defend me, but we must leave the hand-to-hand combat to the royal guards and the police."

As if on cue, Wilson, Claire's exuberant golden retriever, bounded into the room, sat next to Claire, and panted what looked very much like a smile.

Granny tipped her hand toward the canine. "See, he agrees with me. Listen to me. You don't have to be afraid of that woman. God has a wonderful plan for you, and I believe the Good Lord won't let Maurelle touch a single hair on your head. Plus, we have Wilson. He'll protect you, too."

At hearing his name, Wilson swiped the floor with his tail like a mop, his tongue hanging out and his head lolling to the side.

Snorting, Claire rubbed his head. "Yeah, he looks like a great guard dog. Wilson wouldn't hurt anyone."

Granny made a tsking sound. "Except Maurelle. He doesn't like her, either. That dog has good judgment."

"Well, we may not have to find out. Hopefully, Maurelle knows if she resurfaces here that she'll find herself returned to prison immediately. Now, what about this Glenda Halstaff? Why is she coming to help with the Fruhling Gala instead of Mademoiselle Couture?" Claire cocked her head to the side and waited for her granny to give her the scoop.

Granny glanced at the queen mother, who had buried herself in a conversation with the staffer who'd entered the room to remove the group's empty teacups. While the queen mother, who hated gossip, remained occupied, Granny lowered her voice and leaned closer to Claire. "Couture got herself a big score. She's showing a collection at the International Fashion Week in Devon. Guess she's become some bigwig, and her britches are too big for us."

The queen mother overheard this last tidbit and

chimed in, "Now, that is utter nonsense. No one is too big for the queen of Amorley. Be that as it may, we must have the best, and since that is not available, we will take the second-best option—Glenda Halstaff. She's one of the premier celebrity stylists, handlers, and all-around fashion gurus."

Claire whipped her head toward her grandmother. "Did you say 'guru'?" She'd never heard her grandmother use anything close to slang before. Any time her proper, perfectly-coiffed royal grandmother did anything modern, it took her by surprise.

Her grandmother shrugged. "What? I can be hip."

Claire giggled. She raised a hand. "Please. Stop."

Granny and Claire burst into fits of laughter.

After several minutes, Claire wiped a tear away and attempted to regain her composure. "Okay, so when's this Halstaff lady arriving?"

The queen mother glanced at her wristwatch. "She should be here any minute."

As if on cue, Wilson bolted to an alert position and barked nonstop.

A distant voice called from the hallway, broken in part by the staccato click-clacking of stiletto heels that would rival the dissonance of Mademoiselle Couture's legion of minions. "What is that horrible sound? Do they allow beasts in the castle? Is this a petting zoo?"

Claire already didn't like the sound of this woman. She flicked her eyes toward Granny. "One guess who that could be."

Granny rolled her eyes. "Prepare for battle," she whispered.

Before the Thomson girls could discuss the matter further, the new houseguest entered the room two seconds ahead of a disheveled and dumbfounded Nigel.

The queen mother jumped to her feet. "Nigel, what is the meaning of this? The queen hasn't called for her visitor yet. While we are certainly honored and appreciative of the help Fraulein Halstaff will provide, there is protocol in place for receiving guests."

Nigel ran a hand through his hair, smoothing it flat. "Pardon me, ma'am. It couldn't be helped." He sent a pointed, accusing glare toward the fashion titan, then straightened and smoothed his black jacket. "May I present Glenda Halstaff of Maltenstein." He bowed and turned on his heel, leaving the room shaking his head.

Claire's jaw dropped, and she jumped to her feet out of habit. Even though she'd held the title of queen of Amorley for several months, she often felt like a kid playing pretend. This was one of those times. "Pl-please, have a seat." She gestured toward an empty chair.

The woman clapped her hands together two times, and a small army of assistants dressed in grey tweed snapped to attention. With a flick of her hand, the fashion army scattered like cockroaches in a kitchen when the light turned on. She then turned to Claire and let her eyes settle on her project.

Once more, hoping to sound more confident than

she felt, Claire cleared her throat and nodded to a chair across from hers. "Please. Be seated. My grandmother informed me you had been called to assist with the Fruhling Gala preparations. I'm surprised at your willingness to help us, given the current…situation between our two countries."

The militant woman planted herself in the chair across from Claire, her posture remaining rigid. "Yes. Well, I don't concern myself with politics. However, fashion is my passion. I will dispense my vision for your appearance, deportment, apparel, diction, event planning, and gala—the entire thing. Indeed, your life is in my hands. You will listen. The world will love you. You will be pleased. This is what I will do for you," she said, or instead ordered, in a clipped accent.

Granny snorted.

Claire warned her granny before letting her gaze settle on Fraulein Halstaff again. "Wow. Well, that sounds…great. Really. When were you hoping to begin the—" Claire searched for the right word, "operation?"

The woman pursed her lips, and her eyes scanned Claire's attire. "Hmm. Immediately. We must start at once. I see there is much to do. Much to do. We have little time between now and the Fruhling Gala."

"It's still over six months away."

The other woman frowned. "Exactly. Not enough time. Still, we will do what we must."

Panic caused bile to rise in the back of Claire's throat. She swallowed hard and willed it back down.

She could do this, right? Reflecting on all she'd overcome with God's help—multiple threats against her life, a coronation, a wedding—she could survive a glorified spring party. How hard could it be? She just had to plan the gala, maintain a queenly demeanor between now and then, and carry her pregnancy with some semblance of grace to full-term. Easy peasy. Now it was her turn to snort.

The queen mother gasped. "You'll have to excuse my granddaughter. I'm sure she's overcome with deep gratitude for your willingness to help. As I'm sure you've heard, she's pregnant with the country's future heir, and as you can imagine, there is a lot on her mind."

Fraulein Halstaff sniffed. "Yes. I suppose. Well, I must go. Much to do. Much to plan." She cast a sharp stare at Claire. "Get sleep. Eat vegetables. Hydrate. Your skin is dull. We cannot have a dry queen for pictures. We will resume this meeting tomorrow." Her eyes darted toward her minions and clapped twice. The entourage burst into action, and the entire encampment scurried out of the room like a hive of bees following their queen.

Claire stared after them until the room was vacant except for herself, Granny, and her grandmother. Silence filled the space.

Granny cackled, breaking the tension. "She's a fun time, huh? Fraulein makes ole Mademoiselle Couture look like a dream, right?" She sent a teasing glance to

Claire and snickered again.

Shaking her head, Claire put both hands to her temples and massaged them. Somehow within the brief time that the fashion savant had entered her life, Claire had developed a pounding headache. "A dream. Still, I can do this. Right? I have to do it. The only other choice is changing my name, changing my hair color, and fleeing with Ethan and you to another country with a fake alias. I don't suppose that's an option, is it?" She glanced at the queen mother.

"Afraid not, dear," her grandmother replied.

"Right. Well, then, as the Amorley motto says, 'Pressing onward with courage.' I must press onward," Claire declared, though her voice trembled.

# Chapter 2

Ethan squeezed Claire's hand. "Are you sure you don't want me to stay with you for the rest of your appointment?"

She turned her head on the pillow to face him. The hard surface of the examination table that had been temporarily constructed in a spare bedroom caused her to squirm. At twenty weeks, her back had already begun to ache. "No, you have that important business meeting to attend today. I'll be fine. Besides, you were able to see the ultrasound. All that's left to do is measure my abdomen and counsel me on pregnancy's do's and don'ts. I'll fill you in tonight."

He raised a brow. "Promise?" Ethan flashed her a kind grin.

She returned his smile. "Promise. Now, go, or you're going to be late."

Ethan raised her hand to his lips. "All right. Call me if you need anything, and I'll cancel the rest of my day."

She waved him away. "Go." She didn't know who

was worse to hover over her, him or Granny. Neither of them had stopped fussing since they'd learned about her pregnancy.

Ethan rose, leaned over, planted one final kiss on her forehead, and left the room.

A few minutes passed, then a knock sounded on the door.

"Did you forget something? I don't see your briefcase. Maybe it's at your office, I—"

"Excuse me, Your Majesty. It's Dr. Brickworth. Dr. Kimberly Brickworth." She opened the door and crossed the room, extending a hand to her.

Claire awkwardly accepted the gesture and gave the physician a sidewise fist pump. "Pleasure to meet you. I apologize. Thought you were my husband."

The doctor furrowed her brow. "Oh, should we wait for him to finish up? The ultrasound tech completed your study, as you know, and everything looks great there. Still, I wanted to take some measurements and discuss our plan moving forward with you."

Claire shifted again and grimaced. "This kid must be doing somersaults on my spinal cord." She twisted around again. "Sorry. No, go ahead. My husband had to attend a meeting, but he will be at the next appointment, and he got to see the baby on the ultrasound, so he's good."

Dr. Brickworth smiled. "Great." She turned around, rummaged through a small black bag she'd carried into the room, and placed it on the ground. Muttering, she rustled several items around. "I know it's in here somewhere. They call this bag the 'Always Empty,' but as far as I can tell, it's a lie. It's never empty. I can't find anything in it. It holds a ton, but everything mixes together."

Claire chuckled. She had the same bag and recalled a similar conversation between herself and her granny. "I can relate."

"Aha." She yanked out an unraveling measuring tape and thrust it in the air like a banner. "Found it."

Something about the slightly scatterbrained appearance of the doctor and the unraveled state of the measuring tape comforted Claire. This was her kind of person. She imagined they'd have become fast friends if they'd met at the hospital in an everyday situation before Claire had become queen of Amorley.

The doctor stepped closer, placed one end of the measuring tape at the bottom of Claire's abdomen, and stretched the other end to the top, stopping at the fundus of her uterus. "Twenty centimeters. Perfect. You measure consistent with your dates. Everything looks great." She dropped the tape into her bag and righted herself, then extended a hand to Claire and helped her to a sitting position.

Once upright, Claire tucked the ends of the hospital gown around her to ensure modesty. "Thank you for agreeing to come to Evercliff Castle to care for me—and on such short notice." Claire fiddled with the strings of her gown. "I suppose you read in the newspaper that my last obstetrician sold my private health information to the paparazzi." This left Claire on the hunt for someone she could trust. So far, she had a good feeling about Dr. Brickworth.

The physician smiled. "I did read something about that and was sorry to see it. Don't let one bad experience cloud your pregnancy. It's my pleasure to take care of you. When the queen calls, I answer."

Claire's mind flitted back to the day she'd spoken to her grandmother, the queen mother, for the first time and been invited to visit Evercliff. "That's true. What do I need to do, moving forward? I underwent an obstetrics rotation during medical school and an additional month during my intern year, but that was a while ago."

Dr. Brickworth crossed her hands in front of her, and her countenance settled into medical mode. "Of course. I recommend eating a healthy, well-balanced diet with lots of fruits and vegetables."

Claire nodded. "Done."

The physician shifted from one black patent pump to the other. "Make sure you get plenty of sleep—at least eight to nine hours a night."

Frowning, Claire responded, "Less easy to fulfill, but I'll try. What else?"

"Don't forget to take your prenatal vitamins every day, get some light exercise such as walking daily, and keep stress to an absolute minimum."

"Stress?" Claire grimaced. That wasn't going to be so easy. With a Fruhling Gala to plan, a baby to grow, a kingdom to run, foreign relations to manage, and surgeries to perform, *low stress* weren't the first few words that came to mind. Oh, and then there was the pesky factoid that her evil stepmother, who'd been out to dethrone Claire and destroy her life, had escaped prison. No biggie. Claire snorted. "I'll try."

Dr. Brickworth placed a gentle hand on top of Claire's. "You have to take it easy."

Claire frowned. "Right. Anything else?"

The doctor removed her hand and glanced at the chart again. "No. Everything looks good. Don't hesitate to call me if you have any problems, and we will meet once a week for a checkup."

Claire raised a brow. "Once a week? Isn't that excessive? I thought you usually did monthly visits at this stage of pregnancy."

"That's true—usually. However, most patients aren't the queen of Amorley. You're growing the future heir to the crown in there." She pointed at Claire's abdomen. "Can't be too careful. Most of the country and Parliament would agree."

Claire raised her hands in concession. "Fine. Once a week." At least her physician was kind, and she seemed down-to-earth. Maybe they'd even become good friends.

The young obstetrician curtsied before turning to leave the room. She paused as she passed through the doorway and peered over her shoulder. "Remember— take it easy."

Claire tugged her gown tighter. "Right. Easy."

With these parting words of advice, Claire's doctor left the room and closed the door behind her.

It would be fine. All of it. Right? It had to be. She had a monarchy to maintain.

# Chapter 3

When Claire entered the dining room, everyone seated at the table rose. She crossed the room and waved them down. "You don't have to do that every time." They remained standing.

Nigel walked through the kitchen doors, followed by several staffers carrying silver platters. He immediately froze at the sight of Claire. "Your Majesty, please forgive me. We should have had things out and ready before you were seated. My apologies." He bent at the waist.

Claire stood at the head of the table, Ethan to her right and the queen mother to her left. Granny had claimed her place next to Ethan, probably so she could face the queen mother and torture her over breakfast.

One of the waitstaff scooted Claire's chair in for her, and she nodded for everyone else to be seated.

Protocol dictated that everyone must wait for Claire to take the first bite before the rest of the people could eat, so the waitstaff set plates before each person, beginning with Claire. Once each had been served, Claire took the ceremonial first bite, and everyone else dug in.

In between bites of egg, Granny pointed her fork at the queen mother. "Tell me, what's the story on this coalition from Maltenstein? When will the enemy arrive?"

Claire sent her granny, who inhaled her breakfast like a vacuum, a warning glare. "Shh. Keep your voice down. You can't say things like that. They are coming to the castle later today. For all we know, the fraulein has eyes and ears everywhere. Besides, we're supposed to be easing tensions between our two countries. Setting a good example. Providing a warm welcome. All of that. Do you think you can manage it?"

Granny nearly choked on her toast. "Who? Me? I am the picture of democracy."

"Right. Democracy." Claire shook her head and tended to her plate, its contents having cooled. Poking at a questionable jellied substance, Claire paused to consider the soon-to-arrive houseguests. After a few quiet seconds, she looked at Ethan. "What do you think? Am I making a mistake even bothering with this? Is the Fruhling Gala going to be a disaster? It's supposed to be the culmination of the peace efforts between our country and Maltenstein and a celebration of spring, but if things don't go as planned—if they decide they don't want peace—the whole thing could fall apart. It would be a public humiliation to cancel the

Fruhling Gala for the first time in fifty years."

Ethan reached over and squeezed her hand. "Things won't fall apart. You will help orchestrate the best Fruhling celebration Amorley has ever seen, providing a path to peace between the two countries. Everything will work out—you'll see. God won't fail you."

She smiled and squeezed his hand. "You're right. Please remind me of that over the next few months?"

He leaned closer and locked eyes with her. "I will."

The queen mother cleared her throat. "Yes, well, now that we have that matter sorted, there is something else I'd like to discuss with you."

*Oh no*. The last time Claire had heard those words, she'd ended up in a boa constrictor-like dress with Madame Couture barking orders at her. "What is it?" Claire braced herself.

"I thought it would be good for publicity and diplomatic relations if we hosted an event to commemorate the arrival of our foreign guests."

Claire's smile tightened. She'd learned a while ago to hear the entire proposal before agreeing to anything. Otherwise, she might end up on top of a horse giving a speech at a polo match—a sport she knew little about.

"Every year, there is a nationwide dog show. Traditionally, the queen or king attends and acts as the judge of the Best-in-Show portion of the event. You'd say a few words at the opening, smile, and wave for the cameras, demonstrate that foreign relations with Maltenstein are fine, and then help choose the best dog."

"A dog show?" Claire raised a brow. "Like on TV? With ramps, hoops, and the whole deal?"

The queen mother pursed her lips. "No, nothing to that extent. There's no obstacle course. The judges just watch for how the animals move and if they represent the top of their breed. You don't have to worry about any of that, though. You simply state your choice, and all final selections will be fine."

Wilson bounded into the room, barking to announce his arrival. He nearly bowled over Claire, stopping at her feet after bumping into her. His tail swished across the floor, and he panted hard, smiling.

She bent down and patted his head.

Granny chuckled. "We should toss ole Wilson in the competition. I bet he'd take the grand prize."

Ethan laughed. "He'd definitely make a statement."

Claire paused, imagining Wilson's presence at the event. "Right. Perhaps we'll find a sitter for him that day."

The queen mother glanced at her granddaughter. "The dog show is next week. That doesn't leave us much time to prepare."

Claire moved a piece of egg around her plate. "Next week?"

~

The stadium hosting the Amorley Kennel Club Dog Show looked packed. Thousands of fans filled the tiered seats that surrounded the turf-covered ring below. Bright lights overhead cast a glow across the arena that reminded Claire of high school Friday nights. Photographers' flashbulbs popped in an explosion of luminescence, and she rubbed her eyes to keep from going blind.

The queen mother leaned over and whispered in Claire's ear, "Dear, don't rub your face. The public will think you've caught an infection or something. Plus, you'll smear your makeup."

Ah. Right. The makeup. Fraulein Halstaff had arrived several hours before the event on Claire's doorstep with an armament of beauticians. Claire suspected she now resembled a music video icon from the 1980s more than a respectable royal. Still, the celeb guru insisted that she needed a "full face" for today's big event. "Sorry, but it's hard to see between the twelve layers of mascara and the fluorescent lights."

Her grandmother patted her hand. "Your eyes will adjust."

Granny flanked Claire's left side along with Ethan, who had a firm grip on Wilson. She muttered something, but Claire couldn't make out the words. Claire raised her voice, "What did you say? Are you okay? Are you tired? Maybe you should have stayed home and rested."

Granny made a harrumphing noise. "Rested, my

foot. I said this seems like nonsense, but that doesn't mean I don't want to see it."

Claire agreed with her granny but couldn't say so. Not with so much riding on improving relations with Maltenstein. Speaking of which, her eyes scanned the crowd, searching for the country's coalition.

After a few seconds of blinking past the thick layers of goo, her eyes landed on the king of Maltenstein, his wife, the queen, their band of corgis, yipping at their feet, and an entire entourage, including an extensive security detail.

The illustrious Glenda Halstaff and her crew glided past the royal Maltenstein retinue, and Claire noted that they exchanged a quick glance but didn't share a single word. *Hmm.* Halstaff had acted indifferent about politics the other day, but maybe that was all a front.

Granny broke through Claire's thoughts. "Look over there. The fancy-schmancy lady from Maltenstein has arrived."

Claire scrunched her nose. "I saw."

"Hmph. I don't like it. Don't trust that woman. How can she be acting out of the goodness of her heart if she works for them?" Granny hooked her thumb in the direction of the other country's rulers.

"Shh," Claire hissed. "They'll hear you. We're supposed to mend relations with them, not make things worse."

"Pshaw. I don't see why we have to play nice. I say good riddance to the whole lot of them." Granny fiddled with her ever-present rhinestone ball that hung around her neck on a gold chain.

Shaking her head, Claire exhaled a sigh when the introductory trumpet sounded, indicating the beginning of the event.

Granny ribbed Claire. "You're on."

"Ouch. I know, I know." She rose from her seat in the front row and waited for two staff members to straighten her sapphire dress behind her. Then, she stepped forward ten paces and faced the large crowd. Taking the microphone from the announcer, she felt her hands tremble. She'd never grown used to public speaking. It still made her stomach twist.

Raising the microphone, Claire began, "I'd like to welcome everyone to the Amorley Kennel Club Dog Show. This special event has been held for decades, and this year we are honored and grateful to welcome the Maltenstein Royal Family to today's proceedings."

She paused as the crowd gave polite applause.

"I speak for all of Amorley when I say that we hope this occasion will mark the beginning of a long and peaceful relationship between our countries, and I, for one, cannot wait to see what the future holds."

The crowd rose to their feet and cheered.

Claire waved as her grandmother had taught her before returning to her seat. Once seated without any falls or mishaps, her shoulders relaxed. She'd just let a small smile creep upon her face when a flash of raven hair caught her attention out of the corner of her eye.

Turning her head, Claire caught a glimpse of a female figure to the left side of the stadium. The woman wore sunglasses, and her hair was tucked behind her ear. She moved with hurried steps around the stadium's edge toward an exit. The way she moved, almost serpent-like, reminded Claire of someone. No. It couldn't be.

Claire leaned closer to her granny. "Look over there." She pointed in the direction of the woman. "Is that Maurelle?"

Granny craned her neck, her eyes jumping with excitement. She loved drama. "Ooh. Where? Oh, I'd love to see her taken down today. Wouldn't that be something?" Her eyes followed the direction of Claire's finger. After a few seconds, she righted herself. "I don't see her. Are you sure you're getting enough sleep? Maybe your eyes are playing tricks on you."

Claire stared hard at the area where she'd thought her stepmother had stood. The woman had vanished. Maybe her granny was right—perhaps she'd imagined it. "Maybe."

The queen mother cleared her throat. "Your Majesty, the show is beginning."

This was her respectful way of telling her granddaughter, who was now the queen and in charge, to be quiet and pay attention. Claire nodded. "Thank you. Of course." She glanced around the arena, taking in the entire spectacle. Gesturing toward a handler escorting a large golden retriever, Claire asked, "How do they decide the top winner?"

The queen mother fiddled with her white gloves, adjusting the fingertips. "Best in Show. It's called Best in Show. The animal that wins."

"Oh. Right. I've heard of that." Claire smiled. "So, how do they decide who's Best in Show?" She peeked at Wilson, who sat on the ground next to her, his long leash held firmly by a security guard a few seats down. Wilson lifted his head and met her gaze. It almost looked like he'd shared a wink with her. She smirked at him. *Don't get any ideas, buddy. It took a lot of effort to convince everyone to bring you along.*

Releasing a big sigh, he laid his head back down.

The queen mother continued her lecture about the dog show. "There are seven groups of dog breeds that compete, and the animal that receives the most points in their category gets to participate in the final part, the Best in Show. Then those seven dogs take the arena, and the head judge decides the winner, awarding the Best in Show. Points are given based on the dog demonstrating the ideal features of the breed such as size and shape of the head, coat appearance, and many other qualities." Claire's royal grandmother peered at her. "I thought I gave you that handbook on the history of the dog show so you would be prepared for it. Didn't you read it?"

In fact, she had not. With seeing patients weekly at the hospital, ping-ponging to a million public appearances, attending meetings with the head of parliament, and growing a tiny human, Claire hadn't read about the features of each breed—not to mention the million-year history of the Amorley Kennel Club Dog Show. "I did take a look at it." Not a lie. She'd read the cover, the table of contents, and the summary paragraph on the back.

"Hmm." her grandmother sent a disbelieving stare for a few seconds before turning her attention back to the show.

The next few hours passed rather enjoyably, and Claire thought she'd made it through the dog show unscathed.

The announcer and head judge moved toward the center of the arena, and the judge gestured toward the top seven dogs. Their handlers ran the animals around the stadium's perimeter one by one for a final pass. After a few seconds of discussion, the announcer placed the microphone near his mouth. "The judge has made his decision. This year's Amorley Kennel Club Best-in-Show Award goes to Churchill Downs, the golden retriever from Easton Heights. Second place goes to Coat of Arms, the terrier from Scotswood, and third place goes to the chihuahua, Tea Cup, from Ellington."

The crowd stood to their feet and erupted in applause as the judge pointed to each winner.

Clapping her gloved hands, Claire smiled, giving the judge, the winner, and the announcer her best version of a royal head nod.

The judge and announcer nodded in return, and a

sigh of relief passed Claire's lips as something ran over her foot. Her eyes shifted downward, and she gasped.

Wilson bounded over her feet and the well-heeled shoes of several other patrons, then dashed toward the center of the arena.

Claire's jaw dropped. She watched in horror as her impulsive golden retriever sprinted towards the head judge who stood in front of the Best-in-Show champion.

The judge held a sizable floral wreath in his hands, holding it above the winner's head. He grinned and opened his mouth, ready to congratulate the winner, when he noticed the approaching interloper. His eyes widened as Wilson dashed toward him.

Claire gasped. *Oh no*. Wilson had a thing for flowers. He'd loved them ever since he was a puppy. Particularly roses. It had become a sore point between him, the groundskeeper, and the head gardener at Evercliff.

Wilson made a beeline for the wreath. He leaped in the air and grasped the ringed floral arrangement in his mouth. After landing with his prize, he pivoted and ran in the opposite direction toward the arena's main exit.

Heat climbed up Claire's neck, filling her face with warmth. Without thinking, Claire took off after her canine best friend. Even though she wanted to wring his neck, she didn't want him to get lost or hurt. Claire yelled for Wilson several times as she dashed after him. Her heels sank into the ground with each step, and she lost a shoe after a few steps. Footsteps behind her bespoke of the security staff trying to keep up.

After a few minutes, Claire and her team cornered Wilson near the exit, which the kennel club staffers and looky-loos had blocked.

Claire extended her hand. "Wilson, drop it."

The dog doubled down on his claim on the wreath. He hunched his shoulders to the floor, and his bottom stayed high in the air, his tail working overtime. A gleam in his eye told Claire he'd created a fun game and had no intention of losing.

"Wilson," she warned again, "I said, drop it. I mean it. Give it here. That's not yours, and you can't keep it."

He cocked his head to one side, and for a brief moment, she thought she'd gotten through to him. As her shoulders relaxed, Claire took a shoeless step forward to retrieve the Best-in-Show wreath, but he ducked to the right and took off in a flash of fur.

Claire bolted behind him, crossing the entire lawn, her one-shoed legs burning and her gloves becoming loose and floppy as she pumped her arms. He came to a halt just as Claire thought she'd be chasing her misbehaving dog around the arena all day.

One of her security staffers had found a mounted police officer who had used his horse to block the dog, and apparently, Wilson had greater respect for an animal more than twice his size than he did for his owner.

He plopped his rear down, dropped the wreath, and lay down, placing his face between his paws as if he hadn't just wrecked the entire awards ceremony at a prestigious nationally televised event.

*Oh, the press*—she'd forgotten about that aspect of the day. She had no doubt that her picture would be splashed across all the major newspapers tomorrow morning.

Heaving a breath, Claire planted her hands on her thighs and leaned over—very unqueenly. She sputtered between halted breaths, "Th—that wasn't very n—nice, Wilson."

He raised one brow in her direction as if to say, "What did I do?" Then, he returned to his relaxed position flat on the ground.

She grabbed an intake of air. "No, you stay there. By all means, take it easy. I'll clean up the mess you made. No problem."

He sighed, rolled on his side, and began snoring.

"Sounds about right," she muttered. Claire walked over and retrieved the disheveled wreath that now had only half the roses, its shape having morphed from a circle to an uneven octagon. The badge across the middle read, *Best in how*. The "S" had been gnawed off and probably remained somewhere between here and the chihuahua on the other side of the arena.

Super.

She carried the wreath gently to the center of the arena and handed it to the announcer. After a few minutes of apologizing to the judge, who gave her a terse bow, she returned to her seat, hobbling as if on a pogo stick.

As Claire sank next to her grandmother and Granny, she closed her eyes and drew a deep breath, waiting for the commentary to commence.

Her grandmother tsked. "I—I have no words."

Granny leaned closer to Claire and whispered, "That's a first."

Claire snorted, and her hand flew to her mouth. "Excuse me."

Her grandmother pursed her lips. "You are the queen, and although it is no longer my place to tell you how to run the country, I would be remiss if I didn't say that perhaps in the future, it would be best if Wilson stayed home from public events."

Granny chuckled. "You think?"

"Yes, I suppose you have a point. In Wilson's defense, he does love roses." Claire crossed her legs, trying to conceal her shoeless foot.

"Looking for this?" Ethan walked up and presented her with the missing shoe, not unlike a certain prince with a glass slipper.

The wave of nausea that had been building up subsided at the sight of the man she loved. He always had a way of calming her in the middle of life's storms. "Thank you."

He knelt and placed it on her foot like in a fairy tale. "A perfect fit." He raised his eyes to meet hers and sent her a teasing grin.

Butterflies circled within her stomach, and she felt a shiver run down her spine at the touch of his finger grazing her ankle. She locked eyes with the man who had captured her heart and smiled. "I love you. Thanks again."

He returned her smile with a grin that lit up his brilliant blue eyes. "You're welcome." Ethan rose and took his place beside her once her granny made room for him.

Claire overhead Granny cackle to Ethan, "Did you see that? Wilson made his national dog-show debut. Best thing I've seen all day. Certainly, more interesting than all this hoity-toity stuff."

"Shh," Claire hissed. She righted her posture and crossed her ankles as her grandmother had shown her during royal lessons. Then, Claire adjusted her rumpled gloves and tugged them on until they fit smoothly on her fingers. She patted her hair, praying it didn't resemble that poor wreath. *Maybe no one noticed.* After all, there was a lot of activity happening at the dog show. The whole Wilson debacle had lasted minutes at the most, and with everyone focusing on the competitors, maybe no one would remember that the queen of Amorley had raced around the arena like a one-legged goose.

She peered around the arena to ascertain the damage.

Each face her gaze landed upon met hers, many

slack-jawed.
*Okay. Maybe not.*

# Chapter 4

Ethan sank into his chair after his wife had taken her seat at the breakfast table. "It really is not that bad."

Claire stared at the front page of the *Amorley Tribune* and gasped. Even though the dog show had taken place weeks ago, the paper continued to run stories on it.

Today's episode included a front-page photo of Claire chasing after her dog with one shoe on and one shoe off, her hair whipping out of her chignon, and an intense glint in her eyes as if she wanted to strangle someone.

In the picture, Wilson held the ragged wreath in his mouth and had a look of glee in his eyes. Behind them stood several onlookers, including the announcer and head judge, both of whom covered their mouths.

"It is that bad." She dropped the paper and pinched the bridge of her nose.

Ethan squeezed her hand. "Try not to think about it. Today is a happy day. It's your weekly checkup.

Maybe the doctor will let us take another look at the baby."

He had a point. Even though she had access to the medical equipment all the time and could request a glimpse of her baby whenever the mood struck her, she refrained from abusing her position—not only for the sake of appearances and the hospital resources but also because she didn't want to become obsessed with every bit of nuance she saw on the screen. Sometimes too much information wasn't good.

Thinking about the baby caused a smile to tug at the corners of her lips. She opened her eyes and turned to her husband. "You're right. Besides, this whole mess will still be here tomorrow. I'll see my patients, attend my checkup, and meet you at the lake afterward. It will be a good day." See? Look at how far God had brought her. Six months ago, a disastrous photo in the morning paper would have sent her into a tailspin.

Still, a tinge of fear tugged at her heart. She couldn't ignore the nagging feeling that Maurelle was out there in the world, hatching some nefarious plan. No, she would tuck all those concerns away today and focus on the positive—her baby. Today she might find out if it was a boy or a girl, and she couldn't contain her excitement. The last two times the technician had tried to find out the gender, the baby hadn't cooperated. *It figures. All the Thomson women like to keep things suspenseful.*

Ethan scraped some runny egg onto his fork and

took a bite. As he chewed, he glanced at his wife again. "Where's your grandmother?"

The queen mother had remained holed up in her bedroom since they'd returned from the dog show.

Claire's stomach plummeted. "She told Nigel that she wasn't feeling well and requested breakfast in her room."

Ethan gave Claire's hand another squeeze. "She'll be all right. She just needs a little more time to put it past her."

Granny's sweet but sassy voice echoed from the kitchen, "You flatter me."

Claire furrowed her brow. "What's she doing in there? I didn't realize Granny had come downstairs already. I assumed she'd done the same as Grandmother and hid for the duration. Not that my antics would have embarrassed her. It takes a lot more than a dog show turned rodeo to humiliate Granny."

Ethan shrugged. "I didn't realize she was down here either."

At that moment, Granny sashayed into the dining room with her arm hooked in Nigel's. To his credit, beads of sweat dotted his forehead, and his cheeks flushed. Still, a small smile revealed that it wasn't total displeasure having the lovely Thomson elder attached to his arm. The two of them almost looked like a teenage couple caught kissing on the back porch when they were supposed to be doing homework.

Nigel dropped Granny's arm and jumped two feet

away, his eyes wide. He must not have realized that Claire was already sitting at the table. At least, he was shocked but not Granny. It took a lot to shock her.

Claire cleared her throat and smirked. "Don't mind us."

Granny cackled all the way to her seat. "Oh, I won't."

Nigel resumed his usual respectful countenance and straightened his posture. "Forgive me, Your Majesty. We were just…discussing today's agenda. Mrs. Thomson mentioned you wanted to take an excursion to the lake?"

She sent him a grin. "Yes, that's right. After everything that happened weeks ago, Ethan and I thought an afternoon on the water might be peaceful."

Nigel frowned. "Are you certain you won't get too cold? Forgive me for my objection, but it is the middle of winter."

Granny sent Claire a wink and glanced at Nigel. "Oh, she'll be fine. She's a Thomson—made of strong stock. Besides, we're from Boston. You haven't experienced cold until you've endured an American East Coast winter." She turned to Claire. "You two enjoy your day. Nigel and I will…hold down the fort here."

*Nigel*? Since when did her granny have a pet name for the head of the household? *Hmm. Interesting.* Maybe Granny had a few secrets of her own. Claire's gaze shifted between her granny and the nervous butler.

Distracted, Claire tapped her fork against her plate, considering whether to probe the relationship further. After a few seconds, she thought better of it. "That sounds great. Enjoy your day, too."

Granny giggled again. "Oh, we will. We will."

Claire finished her breakfast in silence, ignoring the flirtatious glances exchanged between her granny and Nigel. Happiness filled her heart for the woman who helped raise her. Granny deserved to have someone, but she doubted the queen mother would share Claire's joy over the pairing. Add Granny to the growing list of her concerns.

~

Claire turned her head and looked at the image of her growing baby on the ultrasound monitor. "I can't believe it."

Dr. Brickworth moved the wand around for one last measurement and then removed it. She wiped off the cold, sticky gel from Claire's abdomen and reached out a hand to help her sit up. "Believe it. It's a shame that your husband couldn't be here to find out the gender. When are you going to tell him?"

Claire groaned as she swung her feet over the side of the table. "He wanted to come, but he had a meeting scheduled for months, so I told him to keep it and that he could come next time. He's a busy guy." Ethan juggled helping her run the kingdom as king and working tirelessly at his own business with family dealings in finance and real estate. "I'm meeting him this afternoon, so I'll tell him then."

Dr. Brickworth grinned. "Good. Now, are you taking it easy? Getting plenty of rest?"

Claire flicked at her robe's tie. "Yes. Well, some rest. I mean, I'm trying."

Her doctor sent her a pointed stare but remained silent.

"I know, I know. I'm doing the best I can. Ethan and I will take a quiet stroll around the lake later today. Bundled up, of course. That's peaceful, right?" As peaceful as having a security detail and rascally dog tag along could be.

Her new friend raised a brow, apparently unconvinced. "It's a start." She scribbled something on a prescription pad and tore it off, handing it to Claire.

Claire reached for it, and her eyes scanned the partially decipherable words. She glanced back at the doctor. "What's this?"

Dr. Brickworth turned to her computer and started typing notes about the visit. "It's a prescription. Stop worrying and take a break. Find some peace." She continued typing for a few seconds before meeting Claire's gaze again. "I saw what happened at the dog show."

Claire cringed. "Yeah, well—not my finest hour."

The doctor shrugged. "Perhaps not, but that's not what I meant. Regardless of the day's chaos, you looked extremely stressed. Even before your dog stole the wreath—and the show, the camera panned across your face at the opening. I didn't see any peace there. It's not good for you, and it's definitely not good for the baby."

Claire quickly digested this information before responding, "I hear you." She ticked the items off on her fingers one by one. "Stop worrying. Get some rest, release my fears to God, and find peace. I'll try."

Her doctor smiled and turned off her computer. "Good. I'll let you get changed so you can meet your husband and tell him about the baby. Remember what I said, though, all right?"

Claire tightened her robe around herself. "I will." She appreciated Dr. Brickworth's advice, and they were quickly becoming fast friends. They'd had tea together several times since her last appointment, and she found it comforting finally to have a female friend in Amorley.

As the doctor left the room, Claire pondered this promise. Maybe she could keep it this time. Maybe.

~

Ethan held tight to his wife's hand as they strolled along the trail flanking the lake's edge. The temperature had plummeted over the past week and brought snowflakes, a brittle wind, and the full deliverance of winter.

The lake's usual pristine waters had hardened to a white sheet of ice. The rim of the lake looked thinner than the center, and small reeds poked through the solid mass here and there. Even though it hadn't frozen solid yet, the wildlife had taken the hint and migrated elsewhere for the season.

Claire shivered.

Dropping her hand, Ethan placed an arm around her shoulder, bringing her closer to his body to give her added warmth. "I'll keep you warm." He glanced around and, seeing no paparazzi in sight, planted a gentle kiss on the top of her head.

Claire's cheeks flushed, and the pink tinge only made her look more beautiful. "Promise?"

He grinned. "I promise." They walked in silence with their arms intertwined for several minutes. "How was your appointment?"

"I almost forgot to tell you the biggest news of our lives because I've worried about Maurelle, the Fruhling Gala, and the dog-show fiasco. I'm so sorry."

He gave her a squeeze. "Don't apologize. You have a lot of responsibilities. So, how did it go? Everything good with the baby?"

Claire's small smile widened as she met his gaze. "More than good. I found out the baby's gender."

Ethan stopped and turned to face her. "That's right. I'm sorry I didn't ask as soon as I saw you. It's been a busy day. When you didn't mention it right away, I just assumed that maybe they couldn't tell."

"The baby cooperated with her position, so we got a good look."

Ethan continued, taking her hands in his, "That's great, so what did—wait." He smiled. "Did you say *her*? We're having a baby girl?"

She whispered, "We're having a girl. She's beautiful, healthy, and growing exactly as she should. Everything looks great."

Ethan scooped her into his arms for several minutes, resting in the moment's complete joy. They'd been through so much over the past several months. He wanted to enjoy this pocket of happiness.

As they stood together in a warm embrace, a commotion across the lake evoked Wilson's barking. He became laser-focused on the source of the noise rustling in the trees.

~

Claire's head whipped up, and she hollered at Wilson, "Stop that. Stay. Wait. Sit. Leave it." She shouted every cue that they'd ever used on him. It was no use. The dog ignored all of Claire's pleadings and shot off across the semi-frozen lake toward the opposite tree line. Claire sucked in a sharp breath and held it, panic flashing across her face.

Wilson wouldn't make it to the other side—no way. The distance appeared too far, and Ethan doubted the ice would hold.

Squeezing Ethan's hand, Claire chanted, "Please don't fall in. Please don't fall in."

When Wilson had crossed the most dangerous part of the lake and hope filled Ethan's heart, a cracking sound filled the air. *No.*

Wilson had made it halfway across the lake when the center of the iceberg split and cracked into several pieces. The sweet yet bullheaded dog fell through the ice into the frigid water below. His upper body pawed frantically, trying to swim or grab onto something.

At first, it looked like he might hoist himself onto the remaining solid slab of ice, but after a few attempts, he slipped further down into the water until only his nose and ears remained above the surface.

"No!" Claire released a guttural yell. She turned to Ethan; her eyes widened. "I can't lose him. He's my best friend."

After losing Milo, Claire's first dog, and one of the few remaining members of her family, she might not survive the loss of another animal. Claire ran toward the lake's edge and jumped over a large branch on the embankment. She lunged forward, attempting to reach the endangered animal. "I'm coming," she screamed. All she could hear was his whimper.

~

Before Ethan could stop her, Claire lunged again, and this time her leg landed in several feet of water as the ground below her gave way to a swampy mess. The shock of the cold liquid made her gasp.

Just then, Ethan grabbed her from behind. He put his arm under hers and hoisted her back to dry ground. "Wait here. You can't go out there—you'll sink, too. Then, I'll have to save both of you." Ethan dashed to the opposite side of the lake. He searched the ground for a large stick. After he found one, he used it to pound on the frozen part of the water's edge and create a path to Wilson.

John Rogers, Claire's head of security, called from somewhere behind him, "Your Royal Highness, please wait. We cannot allow you to put yourself at risk."

Ethan ignored the security man's objections and pressed onward. He shrugged off his wool coat and trudged to where Wilson floated, nearly submerged like a canine popsicle. Still wearing his dress jacket, pants, and tie, Ethan scooped the dog into his arms.

Once on dry land, Ethan set Wilson down and draped his dry winter coat across the shivering, soaked furry frame.

Claire ran around the edge of the lake to join them and threw her arms around Wilson's neck. "Oh, buddy, are you okay?"

He shivered in response and stared at her, his ears matted down, his eyes plaintive.

Ethan wrung out the sleeves of his shirt and then leaned down to pick up Wilson once more. "Let's take him to the castle to warm him up. He's not out of danger yet. Wilson was in the water for several minutes, and I'm sure it dropped his temperature quite a bit."

Claire nodded. "I've treated hypothermia several times during my internship. Rewarming can be tricky—at least for humans. I'll call the vet on the way."

Ethan trudged around the lake, returning to where they'd started. John shook his head. "Sir, you could have drowned or been seriously injured. You should have let us go after Mr. Wilson."

Ignoring the chastisement, Ethan hiked up the small hillside to the awaiting car. Despite the driver's displeased look at the wet passengers, including a soaked dog in the vehicle, he held the door open while Ethan slid Wilson inside. The driver jumped in the front seat and started the engine.

Glancing at the driver in the rear-view mirror, he asked, "Could you turn the heat up to high?"

The gentleman frowned but cranked the knob, sending a blast of warm air on Ethan, Claire, and Wilson's faces.

Claire hugged Wilson around the neck and kissed him on the head. She turned her head to the side and found Ethan's gaze. "Thank you for saving him."

Ethan sent her a small smile. "Of course. I'll always go after the people I love."

Wilson looked up at Claire, and his eyes brightened.

Shaking her finger at him, Claire continued, "And you, Mr. Troublemaker, what do you have to say for yourself? You could have died. Don't ever do that again."

His ears drooped a bit, and he tucked his head down as if he knew that he'd made a colossal mistake.

She ruffled the top of his head. "Oh, I still love you. Just don't scare me like that again. You almost gave me a heart attack."

Ethan tilted his head and grinned. "Is it bad that we're talking to a dog as if he's a person?"

Claire continued patting Wilson's soppy head. "Not at all. Besides, Wilson *is* a person—he's my person and definitely part of the family."

"True." Ethan reached over and squeezed her hand; thankful they were warm and unscathed.

After riding for a few seconds in silence, Claire gasped and then groaned.

Ethan frowned. "What's wrong?"

"Just realized I'll have to tell my grandmother about this. I'll never hear the end of it."

Ethan squeezed her hand and lifted it, bringing it to his lips. He placed a soft kiss on top of her hand before reassuring her, "She will understand."

They both stared at one another for a few seconds before erupting in laughter.

Of course, she wouldn't understand. She would be furious. No, not furious, but at least upset that they'd put themselves in danger, and that, once again, Wilson had created chaos that may or may not end up in the *Amorley Tribune* evening edition.

Ethan hadn't seen any photographers following them, but they could be tricky. "All right, she may not understand, but she will get over it. Look at how much has happened and how far we've come."

Claire chuckled. "That's true. I guess if she can forgive me for vomiting all over the front row of Parliament in public, then she can get over a dog in the lake."

"Here's hoping." Ethan released her hand, still smiling, but deep down, he couldn't ignore that Claire's handlers would undoubtedly have something to say about all the recent canine shenanigans. Still, for right now, they were warm, happy, and safe. He'd focus on that for today and worry about the rest of it tomorrow.

~

The queen mother placed her hands on her hips, a very uncharacteristic move. Typically, regardless of the chaos happening, she kept her cool demeanor. Right now, that façade was shot. "What were you two thinking? The Amorley royalty is a laughingstock. And after the nationally—" she emphasized the word *nationally*, "—televised dog show went awry, you've allowed that animal to put you in another ridiculous position."

Claire frowned and shifted her weight. Even though she was the queen and technically in charge of the country, she often felt like a kid regarding her grandmother and Granny. "I understand that, but you weren't there. We had to—"

Her grandmother pursed her lips. "You *had* to traverse the countryside in the middle of winter—and while pregnant, no less? What if Ethan had drowned? Then, what would you do? You're having a baby, and not just any baby. You are carrying the future heir to the Amorley throne. Both of you need to start acting like it."

Claire dropped her gaze, staring at the floor. "I do understand." She stood before her grandmother, still covered in the traces of leaves, dirt, and wet snow that had melted from sitting next to Wilson in the backseat of the car.

Ethan had passed Wilson off to the groundskeeper, who had scrunched his nose at the appearance of the animal covered in lake muck. Then, her husband had jetted upstairs to shower and avoid the uncomfortable interlude with the queen mother.

The queen mother's eyes skimmed Claire's outfit again, and then she sighed. "Perhaps you should go shower and change. You have a meeting with Fraulein Halstaff in—" she glanced at the grandfather clock that had flanked the hallway for who knows how many hundreds of years. "—one hour. She's also coming to help you select outfits for the upcoming Intercontinental Games and the Fruhling Gala activities. Fraulein doesn't strike me as a woman who likes to be kept waiting, even if it's by a queen."

She had totally forgotten about the Halstaff meeting. Yikes. After briefly reflecting on how the Maltenstein-born image-maker would react to Claire's current appearance, especially after the Great Dog Show debacle, she tossed a quick, "You're right," to her grandmother and jetted upstairs.

Exactly fifty-nine minutes later, she stood in the hallway downstairs, checking the grandfather clock once more. This time, she and Wilson were clean, dressed, and prepared for their guest—or at least as ready as she could be. Claire cleared her throat and turned to the queen mother, who stood next to her. "Maybe she's running late."

The queen mother gave a slight shake of the head.

As Claire opened her mouth to continue with her tardiness theory, the clock struck seven p.m., and by the final chime, Nigel appeared with Fraulein Halstaff and her entourage in tow.

"I do not understand the meaning of this. Meeting in the hallway. What's next? Shall we take our dinner outside and eat on a picnic blanket? Perhaps we could forgo shoe wear at the Fruhling Gala and save ourselves the effort of selecting the perfect pair," Fraulein Halstaff poured out a litany of complaints.

Her shoulders tense, Claire drew in a deep breath and exhaled. "I am sorry for receiving you in the hallway—that was not my intention. We had an—" she paused, searching for the best word, "unexpected hiccup today, and I arrived at the castle later than planned. My apologies."

The fashion guru gave Claire a cursory scan and nodded, apparently finding no fault with her appearance. Her lips pursed into prunes. "We have much work to do."

Taking this as her marching orders, Claire spun on her heel and led the entire party down the hallway toward the drawing room. Flashbacks of being ensconced in tight satin and tulle caused Claire's pulse to quicken. *Breathe. It can't be that bad. It's just clothes.* She'd survived everything that Madame Couture had thrown at her, so how hard could this be? Ah, Madame Couture. What she wouldn't give to see her again instead of the fashion drill sergeant on her heels.

The group arrived at the drawing room, and within

minutes Fraulein Halstaff had transformed it into a fashion version of a war room at the Pentagon. Rows of clothing racks covered in hundreds of outfits lined the sides of the room, and makeshift makeup vanities took residence across the entire front of it. She barked orders to her stilettoed staffers.

The shoes must be a requirement when working for a stylist. Claire chuckled at this thought.

Fraulein Halstaff whipped her head around and focused her laser-pointer stare on the source of laughter. "I do not see what is funny. We have little time until the Fruhling Gala and the Intercontinental Games. Not to mention your regular public appearances to attend. You are not ready."

"Well, I suppose that's a matter of opinion because—"

Fraulein Halstaff raised a hand. "No discussion. It's a fact. You are not close to ready." She clapped her hands, and the beehive of activity resumed. Ten minutes later, the staffers stood in front of the clothing racks, dressed from head to toe in all-black pantsuits, each holding their hands behind their backs as if they were ready for a military inspection.

*Whew. This lady defined intense.*

Fraulein Halstaff shouted in Maltensteinian and then pivoted to face Claire. "First, we will get rid of that atrocity." She pointed to Claire's thoughtfully chosen slim black pants, heeled boots, and a smart tweed blazer. Claire loved this outfit. Every time she wore it, she felt like she could saddle up and play the part of queen in the countryside. Mademoiselle Couture had hand-selected the expensive outfit while working on Claire's wardrobe. "I don't think this is that bad. Madame Couture—"

Fraulein Halstaff pressed her lips together in a thin line. "No. It's awful. I don't want to hear that woman's name. Now, please, the time." She tapped her wristwatch.

Despite being the queen of Amorley, Claire shrank in the shadow of the intimidating woman. She hopped into action and allowed one of the staffers to lead her to a changing area they had erected.

After wiggling out of her clothes, she accepted new ones from a stick-straight blonde-haired staffer who wore an expressionless face. Claire smiled at her but received no response. *Well, she's fun.*

One hour and five hundred outfits later, Claire's winter weather and spring wardrobes had been selected, and Fraulein Halstaff's grim expression had softened into a small smile.

As Claire squirmed into the blue tea-length dress that the stylist chose for her to wear to the tea, she called over the partition, "Thank you for your help. I greatly appreciate it."

Fraulein Halstaff barked, "What was that? I cannot understand you when you shout through a wall."

To be fair, it was only a half-wall. Claire twisted her arm around until her fingertips grasped the zipper, and after a few heaves and one long moment of holding her breath, she managed to exit the changing area intact. Fixing her gaze on Fraulein Halstaff, she smiled. "I said, thank you for your help."

The woman pressed her lips together and scanned Claire's ensemble. "Hmm. That really is a lovely gown," she commented, ignoring Claire's expression of gratitude but sounding less sour than usual. She clapped her hands one last time. "I must go. Lots to do. Don't forget about the photo shoot in two weeks. Eight A.M. sharp."

Claire had forgotten about the photo shoot. As a little girl living in the United States with her mom and Granny, the closest they had come to having a family photo shoot was crowding into the mall's photo booth and saying cheese.

"Right." Claire reached out to shake the fashion guru's hand.

Fraulein Halstaff stared at the hand for a brief moment before giving the obligatory curtsy and marching out of the room.

Granny popped in as the last Maltenstein staffer left. "They're a hoot, aren't they? So relaxed and fun. Can't wait to spend more time with them. Kind of like having a party at a funeral."

"Granny, you can't say things like that." *Even if they are true.*

Granny snorted. "Honey, you can say about anything you want when you reach my age."

Claire giggled and scooted closer to her grandmother to give her a hug. She breathed in her perfume, and the tension and fears of the day melted away.

After Granny released her, she grinned. "You ready to grab some food and maybe even a spot of tea with the queen mother?"

Giving her one more squeeze, Claire sighed. "Come on. Let's go."

The queen mother had left in the parade of staffers from Maltenstein, and Claire didn't like to keep her waiting. "All right. Just promise you won't try to sound posh again."

"No promises." Then, Granny cackled as the duo headed down the hallway.

# Chapter 5

Ethan squinted to see the hands on the clock at the opposite end of the room. He'd sat in front of the fireplace with his legs to one side for an hour. At this point, his entire right hip had gone numb.

Claire flanked his right side, and behind them on a glorified tuffet sat the queen mother and Granny. On the floor in between him and Claire lay Wilson. Well, sort of—the family dog had decided to spend much of the photo session stealing pillows off the sofas and chairs, rolling onto his back to show the camera his belly, and running off to the large windows on the side of the room to bark at imaginary squirrels. He must have read Ethan's mind because Wilson rolled on his back as the photographer flashed another photo.

The queen mother sighed. "Perhaps it would be better if we removed Wilson from the photograph this year. He doesn't want to cooperate."

Claire reached forward and scratched the dog's belly. "We can't send out an official family photograph and not include the whole family."

Wilson glanced at his owner and closed his eyes in pleasure.

Claire nodded in the dog's direction.

"Besides, I don't think you'll convince him to move. He looks committed to his spot." As if to show his endorsement of this fact, Wilson sighed and rolled over to one side, stretching further.

Granny chuckled, and even Ethan snickered. The queen mother rolled her eyes. "Fine. Let's get on with it."

The photographer set down his camera and turned to adjust one of the umbrella-shaped stands that embellished the lights. After a quick assessment of his setup, he stepped back and took in the royal family. He put a hand to his chin. "Hmm. If we are going to include your dog, we must persuade him to wake up and look at the camera."

Claire agreed that would be ideal, and usually, Wilson had more energy than all of them put together. Perhaps his puppyness was starting to wane. "I'm not sure what we can do. In case you haven't noticed, he has a mind of his own."

The photographer stared at the snoozing dog and then glanced at his overflowing bag of accessories. "Hang on." He bent down and rummaged around the black sack. "I know I put it in here the other day because I had to take a photo with the duke and duchess of Easton and their new baby. I think if I can just—" He dug further until something made a loud squeaking sound. "Aha!" He pulled out a giant stuffed bunny.

The presence of a furry object that made a fun noise aroused Wilson's attention. He opened one eye and glanced at the toy, lifting his head slightly. Intrigued, he shifted into a seated position and stared at the item.

"That's perfect." He took a few shots and glanced at the digital images. The photographer grinned, and he looked pleased with himself. He squeezed the toy again, and it let out several high-pitched squeals. "Hold still. We're on to something."

Wilson crouched a little lower, and his tail swept back and forth across the floor.

*Uh-oh.* This would not end well. Ethan had seen that stance on Wilson several times—when he'd stolen the food off the table at a crucial dinner, when he'd run through the room coated in mud, and the other day when he'd rushed onto the frozen lake. No—this had disaster written all over it. "Sir, if I may interject—"

The photographer shook his head. "Hold still. I'm getting some good stuff here; I just need to move my angle and adjust the lighting. There's a shadow behind the queen mother." He made a few changes and continued snapping pictures and squeaking the toy.

Ethan spoke again, "I think that's enough of the toy. You might want to put it away. Wilson has a history of—" *Too late.*

Wilson bolted from his briefly obedient seated position; his eyes laser-focused on the faux rabbit.

Claire lunged for his collar but missed. With her increasing baby girth, her center of gravity had shifted. She overcompensated for the movement, tumbling to the ground.

Ethan bent down to check on his wife. "Are you all right?"

Claire rubbed her knee, which had taken the brunt of the fall. "I'm fine. Just a bruise, but other than that, I'm okay. Grab Wilson before he destroys all of the photographer's equipment."

Ethan's eyes darted toward the photographer and their goofy dog.

Wilson clamped onto one end of the stuffed bunny while the shutterbug had a firm grip on the other side. Neither party appeared willing to let go, and the photographer still had a hold on his giant, very expensive camera in the other hand.

"Wilson, let go of the toy. It's not yours." Ethan ran over to grab Wilson's collar, but the dog ducked, evading his grasp.

The canine doubled down and tightened his teeth around one of the rabbit's legs. He pulled harder, and the stitching on the animal couldn't withstand the force. The entire leg departed from the body of the fabric creature, and its stuffing flew all over the ground. Wilson scooted away from the mess with the removed extremity in his mouth, taking in his handiwork.

The photographer's jaw fell, and he dropped the destroyed remnant of the stuffed animal. "Look what you did. I've had that toy since my daughter was three. I can't believe—"

Before completing his tirade, Wilson decided he hadn't finished destroying the family photo session.

In all of the ruckus, the photographer dropped the bunny and the cable attached to the lights.

Wilson took this as an invitation and bolted forward, his sights set on the plastic rope. Within seconds, the cable trailed from his mouth. He pivoted and ran through the door toward the hallway. Since the line remained attached to the light set up and the umbrella, the entire concoction tumbled down like the walls of Jericho. The metal stand attached to the umbrella scraped across the floor, creating a screeching sound effect. The umbrella bounced around like a beach ball, and the light fell to the ground and shattered, sending sharp shards flying all over the floor.

Claire gasped.

Granny cackled.

The queen mother screamed.

Ethan darted his eyes between Claire and the photographer, unsure of what to do next.

Claire waved in the direction of Wilson. "Go get him. He's going to drag that thing all over the castle."

Ethan dashed off in the direction of the rascal retriever, praying he'd catch him before he brought down the entire fortress.

~

Claire sat on the floor, half-amused, half-horrified

at the events that had unfolded. If she wasn't so angry with her dog, she'd be impressed by his speed and determination. What was she going to do? Even though she was the queen and technically in charge of the castle and the country, she hated disappointing her grandmother. A glance at the queen mother confirmed Claire's suspicions—the royal matriarch was not amused.

Claire rose from the ground and brushed herself off. So much for the posh family-photo session. Hopefully, the photographer had managed a good shot before the chaos broke loose. She hurried over to the photographer. He'd taken a tumble himself when Wilson had made his final break. Currently, he remained on the ground with one hand still clutching the torn toy. He stared toward where one of his fancy lights had been, and his face paled. "I am so, so sorry. I don't know what got into Wilson. He's usually well-behaved." Claire put a hand on the man's shoulder to comfort him.

The queen mother snorted—an action incredibly out-of-character for her. Okay, it wasn't so out of the dog's character, but Wilson never meant to cause trouble. He couldn't help himself.

Claire turned her attention back to the photographer. "Are you all right? You didn't get hurt, did you?"

The man glanced at his arms and legs and took inventory. "I don't think so. He just shot off with all of it—the stand, the umbrella, the light. How can an animal of his size exert that much strength?"

"Well, you'd be surprised at how much power a golden retriever has. The other day we were at the Amorley Kennel Club Dog Show, and he escaped a bunch of staff and judges and stole the wreath. He tore that thing to shreds. By the time he was done with it—"

The man met her gaze, and his eyes widened.

*Right. Not helping. Okay. New tactic.* "Uh, I'm sure your stuff will be fine, though. That equipment looks hearty, and I bet it can withstand more force than some silly wreath." She patted his shoulder again. "Seriously, Ethan runs fast, and I'm sure he's caught up with Wilson by now. Don't worry," she said, more so for her benefit, not that she believed it. More than likely, Wilson had ruined all of the equipment, and one of her staff would leak an unflattering photo of the entire debacle. Yet again, Claire would end up front page as failure number one in all of Amorley.

Claire rose and decided she couldn't help with chasing down Wilson in her current condition, so she focused on gathering the scattered remnants of the photographer's equipment.

The gentleman turned to her as they tucked away the last surviving umbrella. "Perhaps, for next year's family photograph, you might leave the dog out of it. Just a thought."

The queen mother made a harrumphing sound.

Claire sent the man a small smile. "Right. I'll keep

that in mind."

At that moment, Ethan entered the room, sweat beading his forehead and his arms full of what remained of the photographer's things. "I tracked him down and salvaged the stand, but most of the umbrella didn't survive, I'm afraid."

The photographer's face flushed, and he started muttering. "Not being paid enough for this. Can't believe it always happens to me, animals running amuck."

Ethan handed over the stand. "Would you like me to help you carry these things?"

The man shook his head. "You've all done enough, thank you. I'll be on my way."

Claire stepped forward. "I can call for Nigel and some staff to help and see you out."

The man raised a hand. "That won't be necessary. You've all done enough." With his parting words, he offered a terse bow and slipped away with his surviving equipment.

The room fell silent, and everyone sat there for several minutes.

"Yikes," Granny crowed, breaking the silence.

*Yikes is right.* Claire cleared her throat. "Well, I suppose that went as poorly as it could have, so at least the royal family photo sessions can only improve from here. Right?" She peered at the queen mother, praying she would forgive her and Wilson.

Her grandmother met Claire's gaze and lingered

there. "Right." Then she gave her granddaughter a small smile.

*Whew.* Even though the day had been an utter disaster, her grandmother still loved her. That held a blessing. Hopefully, tomorrow would be a new day—one in which Wilson wouldn't wreck everything in his path. *Right.*

# Chapter 6

**Whenever she was** nervous, Claire rambled. Today proved no exception. "I don't think it looks that bad. Sure, it's not what you think of when you conjure the idea of royalty, but nothing is perfect, right? Isn't that what we've learned since I came to the castle?"

The queen mother pursed her lips and nodded toward the empty chair. "May I?"

Claire sat in the opposite seat, her usual position in the drawing room. Her grandmother asked permission to sit as a pleasantry, but Claire couldn't refuse her. "Absolutely."

The queen mother tucked her skirt under her and settled in the seat. "Dear, I realize you are ruling the country now, and I do not intend to hurt your feelings, but—"

Claire fiddled with the edge of her dress, rolling the fabric between her fingers.

"—This is not acceptable. That animal's behavior at the photo session was not acceptable. For that matter, neither was his behavior at the dog show. It may be time to consider sending Wilson to live at the country home and visiting him whenever you are on holiday, or your official duties and obligations have been met for the season."

The suggestion hit Claire like a punch to the gut. All the air emptied from her lungs. "I—I can't send Wilson away. He's my family. Wilson doesn't mean to cause all this trouble. He has a good heart and intentions. It's just he becomes excited and overzealous sometimes, and before he knows it, he's in the middle of a dog show ring holding a mangled wreath or a rabbit. Please, please try to understand."

Her grandmother leaned forward, and her eyes became serious. "I understand how much you love him, but you must also consider your responsibilities—to your country, job, and new child. These are also important things that deserve excellence and more time and attention than you may be able to provide with him underfoot."

Bile stung the back of Claire's throat, but she choked it back down. "No. I can't send him away. Please. Give him another chance. I know he can do better. I'll make sure he does."

Claire watched as her grandmother's chest rose and fell while she considered her granddaughter's plea. Of course, the final decision remained in Claire's hands, but she couldn't say she didn't understand her grandmother's viewpoint, and with the way Wilson had behaved lately, she didn't know if they'd have any other choice. Still, the thought of not having him sleeping at the foot of her bed every night caused tears to sting her eyes.

"All right. I'll speak with Nigel, with your permission, about keeping a tighter rein on him, and we will see how the next few months progress. However, time is growing short before the Intercontinental Games and the Fruhling Gala. We need to set a good example and start the festivities on the right foot, so we cannot afford any more mishaps. You understand the importance of that, don't you?" The queen mother sent her a pointed stare.

"Of course," Claire whispered. She didn't want to fail or upset anyone. Not ever. Quite the opposite. She tried to set a good example for her citizens, to make her family proud, and to leave a legacy of excellence, not chaos. But she loved Wilson. Wasn't it worth fighting for the people and pets you love? She didn't add anything else to her argument but tucked her thoughts away until she could speak to Ethan later. He always knew exactly what to say to make her feel better.

Her grandmother patted her hand and then sat back in her chair. "Good. I'm glad we had this chat."

*Yeah. Super glad.*

~

Ethan rolled his dress shirt sleeves up and rested his elbow on the wooden library table, leaning his head against his fist. He looked very un-Ethany. Her husband hardly ever unbuttoned his collar, much less rolled up his sleeves.

Claire smirked.

Raising a brow, Ethan asked, "What? What's so funny?"

She shrugged. "Oh, I've just never seen you like this."

He glanced down at his shirt before meeting her gaze again. "Like what?"

She pointed to his arms. "Casual."

"I'm casual," he argued. "I spend most of my days here going to events or at the office on official business, so I don't have many opportunities for rolled-up-sleeve moments, but I can do casual, as you Americans say."

"You don't do casual. You *are* casual."

"Either way," he continued. "But that's beside the point. I'm sitting here, casually ready to hear what happened."

Claire leaned forward and clasped her hands together, tucking them under her chin. "Grandmother told me yesterday that I needed to ship Wilson off to the country or boarding school."

Ethan cocked his head to one side. "Do they make a boarding school for dogs? Is there such a thing?"

Claire swatted him playfully with her hand. "Would you be serious? Of course, there's not an actual boarding school," though she couldn't be sure of that, "but she does want to send him away to the summer castle. She thinks he's too much of a distraction, and with the baby coming soon and the Intercontinental

Games and the Fruhling Gala, she's worried that he's creating too much drama."

Ethan narrowed his eyes. "Your grandmother used the word *drama*?"

She swatted him again. "No, but that's what she meant. Be serious. She wants to send my dog away, and you and I know he's more than a dog—he's family. I can't just ship him off because he's disruptive."

Ethan stared at her, not saying anything for a few seconds.

"What?" she asked. "I've seen that look on your face before. You want to say something but don't know how to say it. Just spit it out."

He cleared his throat. "Well, I can't say I don't see her point of view." Claire started to object, but he raised a hand. "I don't want to send Wilson away, but I understand how your grandmother feels. He's been—" he searched for the right word, "—difficult lately, and he's not done you any favors with the press. We have the Fruhling Gala coming up, and with how things have been between Amorley and Maltenstein, I don't have to tell you that it needs to go well. More than well."

Claire wrung her hands. "I know that. Of course, I know that. But I don't see how much damage a little dog can do at the Intercontinental Games and the Fruhling Gala."

Ethan gazed at Claire, his eyes teasing. "Oh, you don't?"

She reflected on the events of the past few weeks

and cringed. "Okay, maybe you both have a point, but what will we do when we have the baby? Will we ship the baby off if she starts misbehaving? What if she cries all night long, throws food at people, or takes off running across the room during a photo op? I'm sure she will do that. What then? Should we send our child to another city or country because we don't like her behavior?" her voice shook as she spoke, and Claire jumped up from the table, placing her hand on her hip and waiting for him to agree with her.

"I don't plan to send our child away because she demonstrates normal toddler behavior, but I have to remind you that I spent some of my middle and high school years at boarding school, and the experiences had positive aspects."

Claire stamped her foot. "Agh. You drive me crazy. I can't believe you. Our child's not even out of the womb yet, and you and my grandmother already have plans to pack everyone up and ship them off to who knows where?"

Ethan rose from the table and took a step closer to her. "Now, that's not fair. I'm not suggesting that at all. I simply pointed out that boarding school is not the equivalent of prison, and that maybe we should do something about Wilson's behavior, given the important events coming up soon."

Claire didn't know if it was the exhaustion from the day, the frustration from the poor results of recent events, or worry over the future, but she burst into tears.

"No, you hate Wilson. You hate him, and you want to send him off, and as soon as the baby is walking, you want me to send her away, too." She realized she sounded irrational but could not stop the verbal vomit from pouring out of her mouth. Tears streamed down her cheeks.

Ethan stepped forward and placed a gentle hand on her shoulder. "I don't feel that way. I simply suggested—"

She couldn't take any more of this tonight. Instead of being led by rational thought and common sense, she spun on her heel and sped out of the room. Claire took the staircase two steps at a time and could hardly breathe by the time she'd reached her room.

Granny stood in the hallway, and her eyes widened at seeing her winded, pregnant granddaughter. "Oh, honey. You need to sit down. Come here." She led Claire into her bedroom and made her take a seat on the edge of the bed.

Her gaze scanned the room.

Granny hopped up and crossed the floor, her back hunched over with arthritis. She grabbed a half-filled glass of water Claire had left on her dresser from the previous night. "Here, drink this. You'll feel better."

Claire took a few sips between gasps, and after a few minutes of sitting next to Granny, her breathing returned to normal.

Granny tilted her head, inspecting her granddaughter. "Now, what's got you in a tizzy?"

Claire drew in a deep breath and released it. "Grandmother talked with me, and she strongly suggested I send Wilson away due to his bad behavior, at least until after the Fruhling Gala. Ethan agreed. So, I had a fit."

Granny chuckled. "Oh, honey, you're not sending that dog anywhere. You're the queen. Remember? That means you get to rule the roost."

Claire grinned at her granny. "Do I? It still doesn't feel like it. Most days, someone else tells me what to do, say, wear—everything. Before you know it, they'll probably want to ship you away."

"Pshaw. They can't get rid of me. I'm here to stay. Whether they like it or not." She nodded for good measure.

Claire wrapped her arms around her granny and squeezed tight, inhaling the familiar scent of lilacs from her perfume. "I love you. Don't ever leave me."

Granny turned her head and gave the side of Claire's cheek a quick kiss. "I won't." After a few seconds, she let go of Claire and patted her granddaughter's knee. "Now, apologize to your poor husband. I'm sure he feels awful. He meant well."

She was right, but Claire didn't want to admit it. "I'm sure he did, but he still has to have my back."

Granny smiled. "He does."

Claire rose from the bed and headed toward the door, ready to find Ethan and make up with him.

"Hey," Granny called.

Claire glanced at her and paused. "Yeah?"

Cocking her head to the side, a mischievous twinkle glinted in Granny's eye. "Tell him I'll pinch his head off if he tries to get rid of me."

Claire burst into laughter. "You got it."

Granny grinned. "One more thing."

Claire turned and caught her granny's gaze. "What's that?"

Granny's gaze became serious. "Remember that it's not a great idea to go to bed mad—not letting the sun go down on your anger and such."

"Right." Claire sent her granny a smile, left the room, and went on a hunt for marital bliss and the promise of sweet dreams and a fresh start to a better day.

# Chapter 7

Claire settled into her chair at the head of the dining table. The room had been transformed into a conference center. Nigel and his staff had placed several pitchers of water in the center and glasses at each setting. Two silver bowls of fancy mints flanked the ends, and each seat had a notepad and pen.

Tapping her fingers on the table, Claire waited for the Maltenstein faction to arrive. Her grandmother sat to her right, and Ethan sat stiffly on her left. They still hadn't discussed their disagreement, and even though she knew she should apologize and likely would do it, she couldn't bring herself to say the words. Not yet.

Nigel appeared at the doorway with a small army in tow. "May I present the king of Maltenstein, His Royal Highness Franz Spickletz." Nigel gave a slight bow and then crossed the room, heading toward the kitchen.

Granny sat next to the queen mother, but Claire could still hear her mutter, "Where's ole Hoity-toity Halstaff? Thought she was part of their crew."

Claire hissed, "Shh. They'll hear you. She is from Maltenstein, but I'm sure that doesn't mean she must attend all their official meetings."

"Hmpff. I bet she's in deep. Probably a secret spy or something," Granny murmured.

Claire shot her granny a glare, praying her eyes warned her to say no more. The two countries were practically on the cusp of a Cold War, and she didn't need Granny to light the match. Or start the freeze. Whatever.

The group took their seats, about twenty of them in total. King Spickletz and his wife sat beside Ethan and across from the queen mother and Granny. The king wore a black suit with a dark green shirt and bow tie. Maltenstein colors. Sad, depressing colors. His queen matched her husband in a similarly toned velvet gown that grazed the floor.

Claire cleared her throat. "Thank you for meeting with us and working together to plan a successful event. I hope the Intercontinental Games and the Fruhling Gala will provide a way for our two countries to learn more about one another and foster a positive relationship for years to come."

King Spickletz nodded. "We are pleased to be here."

He didn't look that pleased. His mouth turned down at the ends as if waiting for the next piece of disappointing news to arrive.

"Wonderful," Claire added, turning her attention to

his wife. "Your dress is lovely. Such a rich color."

"It is the only acceptable hue—Maltenstein's color. We like strength in everything. Green is a strong color. Blue, however—" she scanned Claire's bodice, which shone in a sapphire blue, "represents sadness."

Claire's stomach sank. So, that's how this would go. *Fine.* "It doesn't mean sadness. I can't recall that I've ever heard that before. In fact, I believe it means loyalty, trust, and reliability."

Granny jumped in, "Also, it matches her eyes and brightens her skin tone, which is more than I can say for that getup of yours—you look like a tree or maybe a leaf."

"Granny!" Claire stared at her granny. Still, she didn't disagree, but this meeting and upcoming events were supposed to improve things, not make them worse.

Granny opened her mouth to say something further on the matter but closed it.

Ethan gestured to the empty notepads before them. "Why don't we get started?"

Claire sent him a grateful smile. "That's a wonderful idea." She quickly mouthed, "Thank you," before anyone else could see her.

He mouthed back a subtle, "You're welcome."

"We have gathered to ensure that our countries are well-represented at the Fruhling Gala and co-host a successful Intercontinental Games. As you all know, this will take place in the days before the gala, and I hope that we can present a unified front to the world, showing everyone that despite our differences, coexistence is possible. After all, the whole point of conducting the games is to encourage peace."

"We agree with you. What thoughts did you have about the Winter Games?" King Spickletz asked.

Claire opened a leather folder before her and removed the top sheet. "I'll have Nigel distribute a copy of this, but I propose we offer alpine skiing, the luge, speed skating, snowboarding, ice skating, and the bobsled."

King Spickletz gave a slow nod after she read each event. "That sounds agreeable to me. I will, of course, need to present this to our parliament and ensure that they have no objections or other suggestions, but those are acceptable to me. They are traditional sports, and in Maltenstein, we hold tradition and country above all else."

Claire placed the sheet next to her folder on the table. "Very well. I'll also present this to our parliament, and once they approve it, we can finalize the games."

Nigel and his waitstaff entered the room, and the conversation paused. They came to each diner and presented them with a plate filled with traditional Maltenstein dishes—*Roulwurst, Einbraten,* and *Britz.* Claire had learned the fancy names for each dish the night before, but she hadn't bothered to review their contents, so their actual presentation came as a shock.

As a surprise, *Roulwurst* resembled fried intestines from some type of mammal, *Einbraten* looked like pickled beets—or at least she hoped those were beets, and the *Britz* appeared to be mushy peas. Or maybe she had them all mixed up; she couldn't remember what name went with what item. She glanced at Nigel, "Thank you."

Granny didn't hold back, "What is this? It looks like that stuff my grandmother fed to the pigs on her farm."

"Granny, it is most certainly not anything of the sort. These dishes are all Maltenstein delicacies, and we are honored to sample them." She glared at her granny, whom she loved but wanted to strangle at the moment. Still, Granny had a point. The food had caused Claire's appetite to vanish.

She caught King Spickletz's gaze, so she picked up her fork. "What interesting dishes." She poked at the green substance and moved it across the plate. Perhaps if she smooshed things around, it would look like she'd taken a bite. Claire stabbed the sausage-like entity with her fork and tried to cut it with her knife. After three attempts, she sawed off a small piece. Lifting it to her lips, she hesitated, her hand shaky, but not wanting to offend her guests, she popped it in her mouth and moved it around.

Instant nausea washed over her, and a thin layer of perspiration coated the back of her neck. Glancing at Ethan, his face paled, and she suspected he had the same sentiments about the food she and Granny had shared.

King Spickletz's wife prattled on about the upcoming games and the gala and commented on how crucial the coming week would be to both countries.

Claire nodded and smiled, but inside, she wanted to disappear. Okay, sure, she was being overdramatic— but seriously, if she had to chew and swallow one more bite of the Glutenstach—she didn't even know if she was saying that correctly—she would throw up in front of her important guests. Wasn't one episode of public puking in a lifetime enough? *Yes*.

The queen of Maltenstein must have noticed Claire staring at her plate because she paused her chatter about the games and pointed at Claire's Glutenstach with her fork. "That is one of the most delicious things you will ever eat. In Maltenstein, we pride ourselves on that dish above all others. There is an old saying, 'You can't be a Maltensteinian if you don't like Glutenstach,' and it's so true. Eat. You will love it."

Well, now Claire couldn't put it off any longer. She glanced at the queen and nodded, stabbing the brown item with her fork. Bringing it closer to her lips, Claire made the mistake of inhaling. That didn't help anything. It smelled like a cross between stinky feet and caramelized burnt sugar. Not good at all. The putrid scent, the greasy oil dripping from it, and her already pregnant, sensitive stomach created the perfect storm. She'd learned about many things concerning etiquette since coming to the castle, but she could not eat this food. Couldn't do it. Not possible.

Claire cleared her throat and brought the bite to her lips. Slipping it past her teeth sent a shiver down her spine—not in a good way. She chewed and smiled, praying that her face didn't reveal how she truly felt—nauseous.

On the positive side, the wife seemed satisfied with this acquiescence from Claire and returned her attention to the Fruhling Gala plans.

Claire continued to chew on that bite for a minute or two. She found it incredible—the piece would not break down. It wouldn't tear apart; it wouldn't dissolve. That piece of meat held  indestructible properties. Panic filled her chest. What would she do? She couldn't swallow it, or she'd choke. Her eyes darted around the table, searching for an answer. Landing on the pristine white linen lying on her lap, Claire made a quick decision. She slid it off and brought it to her lips as if to dab at an errant piece of food, but instead, she spit the mangled bite of meat into the napkin. Quickly folding her hand around the food, she tucked the ball of cloth and sludge onto her lap.

Glancing around the table, it didn't appear that anyone had noticed. *Whew*.

The rest of the meal continued rather pleasantly, and Claire breathed a sigh of relief when Nigel served dessert and then vanished into the kitchen again. She'd done it. For once, she'd mustered through an important event with no fiascos.

Granny waved at something above the table that kept flying around her head. "What in the world is that?" She swatted again. "A bee? How did that sucker make his way in here? It's not even summer. He should have flown south or hibernated or whatever they do when the weather turns cold. Besides, I thought this place stayed locked tight like a fortress."

The Maltenstein crew's faces twisted into displeased frowns at the idea of an insect intruding upon their meal.

Claire called one of the waitstaff over. "Could you please ask Nigel to bring something to remove the bee?"

The gentleman nodded and left to find his boss.

After a minute or so, Nigel appeared with a clean napkin in each fist, ready to whip them around overhead as if he were a fan at an American football game.

Granny smirked. "I like your style."

Nigel's face flushed crimson, but he looked pleased. "Thank you, but let's see if this works first." He waved the napkins around at the bee, attempting to corner it or coax it toward a window.

After Nigel made several unsuccessful swats, the bee made its way toward Claire. After a few zigs and zags above her head, she raised her napkin to help in the efforts, forgetting that it had already been utilized in another manner earlier in the evening.

As if fanning the flame of a bonfire, she waved it until something launched from the napkin. A missile of half-chewed meat soared through the air and landed on the queen of Maltenstein's chest.

Claire's jaw dropped. *Oh no. Not the Glutenstach.*

The queen's face shifted from pink to blazing red.

King Spickletz narrowed his eyes at Claire.

Granny cackled, clearly enjoying the show.

Ethan gasped, his hand covering his mouth.

The queen mother dropped her glass of water, causing a glass-splintering sound that pierced the silence.

Well, Claire had to admit she'd outdone herself this time.

"What is this disgusting thing on my chest?" The queen of Maltenstein screeched, waving her arms around in the air. "Get it off me. Get it off immediately."

The waitstaff jumped into action, but before they could swoop in and save the day, Wilson bounded into the room and flung himself onto the side of the Maltenstein queen's chair, making a play for the lump of meat. He scooped it in his mouth, ducked down, and tore off toward the hallway.

The dinner guests stared after him, their mouths agape. She was the only one relieved that the evidence couldn't be identified. *Right?*

Claire cleared her throat. "Well, I guess that's one way to deal with it. Good thing we have a dog on staff."

The queen of Maltenstein frowned. She didn't look like she shared Claire's sentiment.

The room was eerily silent as if everyone was waiting with bated breath.

Finally, the queen mother sighed. "Perhaps, we should bring the evening to a close. We've accomplished a lot regarding the Fruhling Gala and the Intercontinental Games. I don't have anything further to add. Do you?" She directed her gaze at her granddaughter.

So, they were going to play it as if nothing had happened. Okay, fine. Claire could do that. "Sure. I mean, of course. Excellent idea," she chimed in with her best hoity-toity accent. Her eyes darted to the Maltenstein queen. "Apologies for the unexpected ending to the dinner. Thank you so much for joining us tonight. We look forward to seeing you again at the final event before the games—the Amorley National Rugby Tournament."

"Hmm. Yes, I'm sure that will be delightful." The Maltenstein queen glared at Claire. "You know, she was right about you."

Claire rose from her seat, signaling that the meal had ended. "Who was right about me?"

The woman didn't answer but continued to glare as she rose from her chair. Her husband followed suit, and the Maltenstein faction waited for Claire to exit the room.

She couldn't help but feel like virtual daggers were

being thrown at her back.

Who could the woman have been referring to? Who was right about Claire? It couldn't have been flattering, given the circumstances. She wanted to ask more questions, but given how the evening had progressed, she didn't want to push her luck.

Claire walked calmly until out of sight of her guests and then took the stairs two at a time until she reached the top. Then she dashed down the hallway and into her room as best she could. She couldn't wait to lie down. Her back ached, her feet hurt, and her legs had started to swell. Also, her head started pounding when the mangled piece of meat had landed on the queen of Maltenstein's chest. Ugh. She rubbed her forehead as if she might erase the evening's events from her memory. Nope. Still there. It all had happened.

She slid out of her uncomfortable dress and into her cozy pajamas. Sliding under the covers, Claire pulled the blanket up to her chin and closed her eyes. She whispered a quick prayer, "Dear God, if you could make the rest of the week and the rugby match go smoothly, that would be great." Then, she drifted off to sleep with images of dogs chasing wreaths and chunks of meat dancing in her head. Not quite as efficient as counting sheep, but it would have to do.

# Chapter 8

The month flew by, and before Claire knew it, the day of the rugby match arrived.

Ethan loved rugby, and he hadn't stopped talking about getting to watch some of the top players on the field, or the pitch as Ethan called it.

Claire glanced over at her husband, a nagging thought that something might ruin the event circling her mind.

The corners of his mouth tugged downward.

"What's wrong?" Claire shifted in her seat in the front row. Today marked her first official act as the Amorley National Rugby Union Patron, a distinction previously held by her father, the deceased former King of Amorley, Alexander Evercliff. Ethan had spent weeks tutoring Claire on the finer points of rugby. Still, his crash course on rugby etiquette and rules of play had been brief.

"Nothing. I want today to go well for you—for us. That's all." Ethan reached over and grabbed her hand, giving it a squeeze.

She squeezed it back and sent him a smile. "It will. I'm choosing to believe in a good outcome and have hope. Plus, you did a great job teaching me everything I need to know about rugby. Right?"

He grinned. "Right."

Granny settled in on one side of Ethan while the queen mother flanked Claire's other side.

Granny snickered. "I love you, dear, but the amount you know about rugby could fit into this handbag." She patted a red velvet handbag that matched her monochromatic red tracksuit—okay, it wasn't precisely a tracksuit, but it certainly leaned that way.

Claire grinned and glanced down at her ensemble for the day—a cerulean waistcoat, slim pants, and loafers—the only part of her apparel she enjoyed because they were comfortable and reminded her of the slip-on shoes she often wore during surgery. She also wore a hat with a loopy wire and a bunch of lace attached to it. Fraulein Halstaff had called it a fascinator. Everything on her body itched and felt too tight.

At least Granny looked comfortable. She chewed on a piece of gum and smacked, causing a cacophony of murmurs from the Maltenstein group behind them. Her granny didn't notice but chomped away and leaned closer to Claire. "To tell you the truth, I'm excited to see this match. I love the stripe thing on their uniforms, but it looks a little like they are working in prison."

"Granny!" Claire sent her grandmother a hard

stare.

Granny raised her brow. "What? I'm kidding. Everyone needs to lighten up around here."

Closing her eyes, Claire drew in a deep breath. Today would go well. No fiascos would happen. It had to go smoothly—it just had to.

Ethan must have sensed her anxiety because he reached over and squeezed her hand. "It will be all right. Besides, Granny isn't wrong—they resemble a prison-yard motif."

Claire's mouth cracked into a small grin. She leaned closer to her husband, inhaling the musk of his cologne, and her heartbeat quickened. He still had quite an effect on her. "Very funny," she whispered, letting her eyes drift upward.

He stared deeply into her eyes and wrapped her in the warmth of his gaze. At least, no matter what crazy things happened in the world, she could rest in the knowledge that she had the love of a wonderful man.

Granny leaned over once more. "Where's all their equipment?"

Claire frowned. "What do you mean?"

Granny pointed toward the players on the pitch. "None of them are wearing any helmets or shoulder pads. They're going to get mangled out there."

Ethan jumped into rugby educator mode. "That's what they do. There are no major pieces of equipment. It's an intense sport. The ball is passed behind the player to the other teammates. They aren't allowed to pass it forward. That's what makes it challenging."

Granny scrunched her nose. "How many times can they pass that ball thingy around?"

Ethan was in his element. "As many as they want. The rules state that players cannot block the person running, and everyone can tackle and carry the ball."

Granny scowled. "You mean there aren't any MVPs?"

Now it was Ethan's turn to look confused. "What's an MVP?"

"Most valuable player. Don't you have that here?" She snickered.

"Well, there are prominent rugby players, but that's what makes rugby so great—everyone has a chance to carry the team."

Granny stared hard at the pitch. "Which ones are our guys?"

Ethan pointed toward the pack of men wearing blue and white striped shirts. "We are huddled on that end of the pitch. The green and white striped team represents Maltenstein."

The head ref and the game announcer huddled together and then walked toward Claire. The referee gave a polite bow, as did the announcer, before launching into his request, "Your Majesty, I believe it is about time to start."

"Of course." She rose to her feet and smoothed her jacket before following behind them across the pitch. At least this time, she didn't have to worry about sinking a heel into the grass. She'd also decided to leave Wilson at home, as much as it pained her, but given his recent track record, she didn't want to chance it.

Once they'd reached the center of the pitch, the announcer handed the microphone to Claire.

She gripped the handle of it, her knuckles turning white. At least this time, she wasn't speaking from atop a horse. A brief mental flashback to the debacle that ended in a microphone encased in horse droppings caused Claire to shiver. That wouldn't be the case this time. Nope. Not happening. She cleared her throat. "I'd like to welcome everyone to the Amorley National Rugby Match."

The crowd collectively gave her a blank look, and Claire wondered for a moment if she'd accidentally taken the pitch with toilet paper stuck to her shoe or something. She glanced at her feet and then at the announcer.

He stepped closer. "Ma'am, I don't believe the microphone is on. Try this switch here." He gave the side of it a flick, and it squawked.

She winced. "Thank you," her voice boomed across the arena. Trying to steady her nerves, she swallowed hard before continuing, "As I said, thank you for coming today and supporting this wonderful event. I know that rugby has a longstanding history with Amorley and that my father was a devoted patron of the sport. I hope to follow in his footsteps and continue his legacy of encouraging national pride while crossing borders with international goodwill through sportsmanship." Her lips and fingers had gone numb, but she pressed onward through her speech. She hated—no loathed—public speaking, but she was determined to do an excellent job in her role as queen of Amorley, and she would not fail.

The crowd rose to its feet and joined in rousing applause, filling the stadium with excitement.

Claire handed off the microphone to the announcer and headed back to her seat, determined to end her speech on a high note. Once she'd rejoined her family, Claire became fixated on the game. It still held much that she didn't understand despite her hours of tutoring by Ethan. But by the end of their last session, he'd boosted her confidence to the point that she could pass a test on the subject, even handle the game post-mortem with some degree of savvy.

Typical rugby games lasted about eighty minutes but often lasted much longer, even up to two hours. After a fifteen-minute halftime and a few short delays for minor injuries, the games remained tied at thirty-five points each when the referee made a call about a forward pass.

Claire's granny shot up from her seat. "Are you blind, ref? What is with that call? You need glasses."

The entire row and several sections of people behind Claire turned in unison, as a single organism, toward the direction of the heckling.

Claire dropped her head closer to Granny. "You can't do that here," she hissed.

Granny arched a perfectly drawn-on, ruddy-brown brow. "Do what? State my opinion on the absolutely—" she raised her voice even louder, "—horrible call that guy just made?"

"Granny! Stop. It's not appropriate to disagree with the referee at a rugby game, and even if you do, you definitely don't say it out loud, much less shout it."

Rolling her eyes, Granny let a puff of air escape her lips. "Pshaw. I don't care what all these highfalutin people say. I'll think what I think and say what I say."

Claire pinched the bridge of her nose. A vise grip had formed around her forehead, and she could feel it squeeze tighter with every heartbeat. Dropping her hand, she begged her, "Please. Don't say anything else about the referee for the rest of the game—for me. Pretty please?"

Granny grumbled, "Not making any promises." To her credit, though, she didn't make another peep for the rest of the game.

With no time remaining on the clock, Claire held her breath as the Amorley team attempted a 2-point conversion after scoring.

The Amorley player reared his leg back and kicked the ball over the bar. As it floated toward the crossbar, the crowd became still and silent. She reminded herself of the etiquette rules Ethan had told her. It still seemed odd that they didn't try to distract the other team when making an attempt for points—so different from American football. The rugby ball landed squarely between the posts, and with two points added to the final score, the Amorley National Team clinched the victory.

The crowd jumped to their feet, cheering respectfully for the win. That is, until the referee raised both arms above his head, indicating the need for a medical doctor.

Claire raised her hand to her forehead, shielding her eyes to see the problem. She noted the player who'd made the kick had dropped to the ground. Claire leaped from her seat and, without giving it a second thought, ran across the pitch as fast as her pregnant legs would carry her. She arrived at the scene, winded but ready to help. "What happened?"

The player lay on his back, his right leg bent at the knee and drawn up to his chest. He clutched his right ankle and winced in pain. "I don't know," he groaned. "As always, I kicked the rugby ball, but when my foot came down, I felt a pop in my ankle. I don't think I can walk on it."

Claire glanced at his foot and then met his gaze. "Is it all right if I take a look?"

He grunted out a small yes.

She dropped to the ground and carefully took his foot in her hands. It had started to swell, and she also noted some bruising. After examining it and testing the ligaments for a few minutes, Claire looked at the player again. "It's probably sprained, but you need an x-ray and possibly an MRI. You'll have to wear a walking boot or a brace for a while, too. Definitely no rugby."

"Not what I wanted to hear. Your Majesty," he added, almost embarrassed that he'd forgotten at first who had examined him.

She waved away his formality. "Right now, I'm Dr. Thomson. You don't have to do that. I just want to ensure one of our nation's top players is cared for." She shot her gaze to the referee who stood nearby. "Could you call an ambulance to take him to the hospital to be on the safe side?"

The referee gave a slight bow and agreed, then headed to the side of the pitch to tell the announcer to send the ambulance over.

Within minutes, the medics loaded the gentleman onto a stretcher and into the ambulance.

Claire brushed off her outfit—remnants of grass and dirt from the pitch. The crowd gave polite applause that the player appeared okay and that their queen had saved the day. She gave an embarrassed nod and pivoted to return to her seat. As she neared the royal area, she heard someone behind her say, "Game ball. Catch." Spinning around, she saw a rugby ball flying toward her head. Her eyes widened, and without thinking, Claire ducked.

Unfortunately, the queen of Maltenstein's wife was behind her and directly in the path of the hurling ball. The woman's reflexes failed her, and the ball smacked the queen in the face. Hard.

Claire's hand flew to her mouth, and everyone else gasped.

The immediate crowd surrounding them craned to see in her direction.

The Maltenstein queen's face transformed from pale to red to close to the color of an eggplant within seconds. Okay, an exaggeration, but it didn't look good. Her right eye and nose had doubled in size, and Claire bet that the queen would have a shiner tomorrow.

*Super*. Just what she needed to have happen today. The pièce de résistance

to the match. Claire rushed over to the woman and bent down. "That was a bad hit. I am so sorry. I didn't mean to duck. It was just sort of a reflex thing." She lifted her hand to examine the woman's cheek. "Here, let me see if you have an orbital fracture."

Before Claire could touch the woman's face, the lady jumped back at least a foot and screamed, "Leave me alone. Don't even think about putting this on me. This place is cursed. Look at everything that has happened—first, your dog runs amuck, then you shoot disgusting food at me, and now you've ruined my face." She waved her hand at her nose. "How do I preside with my husband over the Intercontinental Games and Fruhling Gala looking like this? Huh? What do you propose I do?"

"Well…" Claire scratched her head. The tight chignon the queen mother had insisted she wear pulled her eyebrows back, contributing to her head pounding. "Maybe it won't be so bad. Still, you should go to the hospital so that we can get some x-rays. You could have a serious fracture that could affect your vision. Why don't you let me call for another ambulance?"

The woman swatted in Claire's direction, and her voice became sharp. "I am not getting in one of those hideous buses and going to your hospital. One can only imagine what terrible things your staff would do to me there. No. I will go home early and have my staff tend to it." She rose from her seat, ignoring Claire's plea to sit and receive medical attention. The entire Maltenstein faction trailed behind her.

In her perfect timing, Granny chimed in, "Well, that was the cherry on top of this day."

Tears filled Claire's eyes and started to spill over. She couldn't fall apart in front of everyone—it was very unqueenly. *Pull it together*. She drew a deep breath and held it for a few seconds before releasing it. At least she'd survived the Maltenstein visit. One way or another, they were heading home.

A pit formed in Claire's stomach as she realized that the next time she would see the bruised and battered queen of Maltenstein would be at the Intercontinental Games and the Fruhling Gala. She'd be on their home turf. If things had gone as whacky as they had here, she could only imagine what lay ahead.

Ethan reached over and took her hand. "Let's go home. Everything will look better after a good night's sleep. All of this will be forgotten by the time we arrive in Maltenstein."

Claire appreciated her husband trying to cheer her up even if she didn't buy it. She didn't have the energy to argue with him, so instead, she rose to her feet, signaling the event's conclusion. "I'm sure you're right."

As she walked out of the stadium, one thought bathed her brain—In her present state, she wasn't sure she could continue juggling everything. All the balls she'd had in the air had come crashing down, starting with the one that landed with a smack on the queen of Maltenstein's face. She didn't know whether to laugh or cry. After a few deep breaths, Claire rolled her shoulders back and attempted to lead the charge out of the stadium with the confidence of a queen—though she still hadn't convinced the most important person of her ability—herself.

# Chapter 9

A knock rapped on Ethan's door.

"Come in," Ethan called from his seat by the fire. He'd called Michael earlier that morning and had been expecting his visit.

Michael, Ethan's best friend, stepped through the door, shrugged off his jacket, and hung his coat on the rack by the door. He shut the door behind him and crossed the room, sinking into an empty armchair beside Ethan. "Are you certain you want me to come along on this trip?"

Ethan rubbed his hands together and then opened them toward the fire to warm them. "Of course. You're my best mate, and I need your help keeping the Intercontinental Games and the Fruhling Gala peaceful. I don't trust the Maltenstein faction, and with Claire due at any moment, I need extra eyes and ears to ensure King Spickletz doesn't do anything underhanded." Glancing at his friend, he asked, "Would you like a cup of tea? It's freezing out there."

Michael blew on his hands, trying to warm them.

"Sure."

Leaning forward, Ethan busied himself by pouring two cups of hot water from the electric kettle on the table beside his chair. He dunked a tea bag in each cup and added a spoonful of sugar.

Michael took the cup of tea from Ethan and raised it to his lips but paused before taking a drink. "I suppose I can move some appointments on my calendar for next week and come with you. Though, I can't imagine what trouble the Maltenstein royal family might cause at a major international event."

Ethan settled back against his chair and took a cautious sip of hot liquid from his cup. "I've learned not to underestimate anyone. After the way Maurelle behaved leading up to our wedding and then the scandal surrounding the coronation, I'm not leaving anything to chance."

Michael leaned forward and placed his drink on the table between the two chairs. He rested his forearm on his thigh and frowned. "You're forgetting something."

Raising a brow, Ethan asked, "What's that?"

"God is in control of all of this. He has His hand on it and will protect you and Claire. You will raise the heir to the throne. As long as you seek Him, He will take care of you. Always."

Ethan sent his friend a grin. "You're right. Sometimes I forget that I have very little control over my life. I think I have to handle everything. Thanks for the reminder."

Michael reached over and gave Ethan a friendly slap on the shoulder. "Anytime. Now, what do I need to pack for this excursion? A million dress shirts? Several hundred tuxedos?"

Ethan chuckled. "No, you need to dust off your skis—if you remember how to use them. He slapped his friend on the back.

Michael frowned, feigning insult. "I cannot believe what I'm hearing. If you recall, I won the university's downhill-skiing competition every year and broke the university record during our final year. If you need a reminder, I can dust off the trophy in my office and pack it with my tuxedo."

"Yes, yes, I hear you. No need to drag that rusty, rickety thing out. I was there when you cheated and beat me on the slopes."

"I did not cheat. The announcer had shouted to start, and the fact that you and the other competitors didn't hear it was on you. Perhaps you needed to have your ears cleaned." Michael smirked.

It had been like this throughout their friendship. Both bantered and sparred back and forth, but Ethan didn't doubt that Michael would do anything for him. He was in many ways closer to him than Ethan's brother.

Ethan sent back a smirk. "Oh, and as an added incentive, Claire's new friend—her obstetrician, Dr. Brickworth—will be there."

Michael's face transitioned from pale to crimson

within seconds. "Why would that matter to me?"

Ethan shrugged. "Just thought you might want to know. I noticed the two of you chatting at the rugby game, and you looked friendly. Quite friendly."

Michael shifted his weight and fiddled with his tie. "Can I not speak to a beautiful woman without creating an inquisition?"

Ethan snickered. "So, she's beautiful now. I thought you hardly noticed her. Interesting."

Michael gave his friend a playful punch. "Don't start. I was being polite at the rugby match. However, if she should appear at the Fruhling Gala and need someone to keep her company or dance with her, I could be forced to oblige—out of duty, of course."

Ethan laughed. "Of course. I'll tell Claire of your great sacrifice for your country as a dance partner and seatmate at the Fruhling Gala."

"Absolutely." Michael grinned, his eyes twinkling.

Taking the final sip of his tea, Ethan glanced at his longtime friend. "Thank you for stopping over. I needed the entertainment, especially after the catastrophe at the rugby game."

"Anytime. Well, I'm off." Michael rose and stretched his arms overhead before righting his suit jacket. He quickly slapped Ethan and headed toward the door with Ethan behind him.

"I suppose I can't procrastinate my work any longer, then. I have a meeting later today about the gala and some things to finish at work. Plus, my father called and wants me to stop over and discuss some urgent parliament matter."

Michael opened the door and paused. "Are things better with your parents and brother? Everyone getting along?"

Ethan shrugged. "As good as can be expected. We have a family dinner at least once a month, and I phone my parents weekly to check in with them." Things used to be much tenser, but thankfully, since the wedding and coronation, his relationship with his parents had improved tremendously. It didn't hurt that he'd married royalty, even if his father had initially protested the match due to old quarrels.

Michael raised a brow. "Have you talked to Richard lately? How are things with him? Is he still with Abigail?"

Shoving his hands in his pockets, Ethan rocked back on his heels. "We're civil. He invited me to lunch the other day, and that went well. We do fine if we avoid the same romantic interest and anything involving competitive sport."

Michael chuckled. "I see. Are they all coming to the Intercontinental Games and the Fruhling Gala?"

"No. My mother is upset about it because she wants to hobnob with the royalty and wear fancy clothes, but my father and brother both have too much work right now to step away. Parliament has been taking more and more of my father's time, and honestly, he's not the biggest fan of Maltenstein. I think the idea of a trip there doesn't appeal to him."

Michael nodded. "Right. Well, call me if you need reinforcements. Otherwise, get ready for your trip to the Grand Royal International Hotel at the foot of Zughorn mountain." He spread his hands as if offering a showcase prize on a game show.

Ethan snorted. "Can't wait." He didn't doubt that the scenery would be beautiful and that, in theory, spending time away at an exciting destination with his gorgeous wife before they became a party of three should thrill him. Still, he couldn't shake the impending dread that something terrible would happen—something much worse than speech notes fluttering out a window or wild carriages taking off down a lane.

As he shut the door behind Michael, he sent up a silent prayer for protection from whatever may be coming his and Claire's way.

# Chapter 10
## April

As Claire watched Nigel heave the final pieces of luggage on the back of a horse-drawn sleigh, she tilted her head. "Now, tell me again why we must traverse the mountain as if we've entered a 1930s Hollywood film or crossed a prairie in the late 1800s?"

Granny put a hand on her hip and frowned. "I don't know how you expect me to get into that thing. The footstep is a mile high, and even though I have a new hip, it won't lift my leg that high."

Nigel grunted as he tossed the last suitcase on the pile and turned to face the Thomson ladies. "Your Majesty, I realize this is not the ideal way to travel, but given the terrain and the past week's snowfall, the sleigh provides the safest way to get you and all of your things to the top of the mountain."

Granny shifted her weight. "Hmpff. That's another thing. Why do we have to stay at the top of the mountain? As far as I can tell, that hotel at the bottom—what's it called? The Grand Royal Something or other is the fancy-schmancy place to stay. Why are these Maltenstein people shacking us up on the hillside? Are they trying to hide us away?"

The Maltenstein liaison turned to Claire. "Certainly not, Your Majesty. Not anything of the sort. As you know, all the major media outlets will feature the Intercontinental Games, and journalists will station themselves at the lodge near the events. Most of the Intercontinental Games take place or start up there, so staying at the lodge provides the perfect location for speaking with the press and overseeing the games. Once everything has concluded at the end of the games, we will assign you to the premier suite in the Grand Royal International Hotel."

"Right." Claire glanced at Ethan and the queen mother. Even though she preferred scrubs to ballgowns, she wouldn't classify herself as outdoorsy. She wrapped her wool peacoat tighter against the cold mountain wind. Snow flurries swirled around her face, landing sharp kisses on her cheeks. "Up to the rustic mountain lodge it is, then."

Nigel helped Granny, the queen mother, and Claire into the second row of the sleigh, and then Ethan took a spot in the rear.

A faint chorus of a favorite Christmas carol played through Claire's mind, causing her to chuckle. She drew a deep breath, sniffing the cold. "I can't believe there's this much snow in the spring. Imagine what it looks like during Christmas."

Granny sent her a half-smile. "I don't need to imagine. It's like this but double the white stuff."

Even though she considered herself more of a summer girl, Claire had a soft spot for a new snowfall, even though the extent of her knowledge about skiing or any winter sport ended at shopping at a sporting goods store for a bulky coat and boots. Still, the chance to see snow-covered trees, drink wassail, and smell the fresh cold air every day couldn't help but put even the most miserly of people in a pleasant mood. She bet even Maurelle wouldn't resist a cup of hot cocoa or two.

Claire smiled at the thought of her and Maurelle sharing a cup of hot chocolate and bonding over the Fruhling celebration—a nice thought but not likely to happen.

Granny glanced at her with narrowed eyes. "What has you grinning like that? It's as cold as a popsicle on a June day."

Claire shook her head. Granny had a way of doling out sayings that made little logical sense but still conveyed her point. "I'm excited to spend time with my family. That's all."

Granny reached over and squeezed Claire's gloved hand. "Me too. Even if this crazy place turns my bones to ice."

Claire rolled her eyes. "I think you're exaggerating. Here." She reached down, grabbed a blanket Nigel had left at their feet, and tucked it around her granny's lap. She raised a brow and caught her gaze. "Better?"

Granny smiled. "Better."

The queen mother chimed in, "What we need to concern ourselves with is not the weather but the Intercontinental Games that start tomorrow. Remember that you have to give a speech at the opening ceremony."

Claire swallowed hard. *Ugh. Public speaking.* Why did this job expect so much of her? Why couldn't she just smile and wave and let them take her picture? Oh, who was she kidding? Most of the time, she or Wilson messed that up, too. "Uh, yeah. I mean, yes. The speech. I haven't forgotten about it." It wasn't a lie. She hadn't forgotten that she had to talk in front of the entire competitive assembly, dignitaries, and the national and international news. She had, however, shoved the anxiety-inducing thought to the back of her mind, burying it under some old boxes in the attic of her thoughts.

As Claire's pulse quickened with the discussion of her big speech, the sleigh pulled away from the lodge. They rode up the mountain in silence for several minutes. When they finally arrived at the top, the wind blew harder, and little icicles clung to Claire's eyelashes.

"We're here," the driver announced.

Claire turned to Ethan. "It feels at least twenty degrees colder up here."

Shivering, he nodded. "Blame the wind chill. It's going to be icy on the slopes this week. Hope there aren't a lot of accidents."

Claire hoped for the same—not that she didn't enjoy practicing medicine—she loved it. However, this trip required her to perform her royal duties and make a good impression on the world for the sake of her country. There wouldn't be much time to chase down the mountain after patients to reset their bones.

The sleigh stopped, and Ethan glanced at his wife, sending her a smile.

Claire felt a cramping pain in her abdomen and grabbed it with both hands. "Oof."

Ethan frowned. "Contraction?"

She held her breath through the discomfort, and as it eased, she released the air she'd been holding. "Yeah. Dr. Brickworth examined me before we left, and she said they were Braxton-Hicks contractions. That's the second one today. False labor pains."

Her husband's brows furrowed. "You need to take it easy. We still have much ahead of us, and you and the baby need rest."

"You're right." Claire couldn't muster the strength to argue with him; besides, she agreed. She didn't want to go into labor while parked on this mountain.

Nigel climbed down and stood beside Claire's side, extending a hand to her.

She placed her hand in his. "Thank you, Nigel." Hoisting herself up and down any type of step proved more difficult with each passing day as she carted a bowling ball in her belly everywhere she went. "Oof," Claire groaned as she landed on the ground. Putting a hand to her low back, she managed a discreet stretch. It probably wasn't very queen-like, but she didn't care. Everything hurt—her feet, her ankles, her back.

Ethan descended from his seat and scooted up next to her. "Are you certain you're all right?"

"I'm fine except for feeling like I'm about to pop." Claire rubbed her belly with her free hand.

As she stepped down from the sleigh, Granny muttered, "You look like it, too."

"Thanks a lot," Claire tossed a smirk at her mischievous grandmother.

The group walked from the sleigh across a charming, stony path to the large, rustic lodge. Snow capped the roof and eaves, and little white lights outlined the frame of the building as well as each door and window. The radiance from them peeking through the snow cast a warm glow. "How cozy." Claire glanced at Ethan and sent him a smile.

He reached over and squeezed her hand. "Yes, it is."

Claire frowned. "Too bad we'll be spending most of our time working."

Ethan eyes flicked toward the building ahead, and he waited as Nigel held the door open for them to enter. Once inside, Ethan peered at a massive fieldstone fireplace at one end of the room containing a roaring fire. In front of it sat an oversized green velvet couch. "Wow, the Maltensteins know how to go all out, don't they?"

Claire's eyes scanned the room, and she sucked in her breath. Overhead hung the most enormous crystal chandelier she'd ever seen, and the walls were constructed from logs, but somehow, the arrangement made it look more like a luxury resort than a log cabin. "They sure do."

Ethan turned to her, and a smile tugged at the corners of his lips. "I have a surprise for you."

She tilted her head. "You do? What is it?"

He stepped closer, pointed at an overstuffed chair, and lowered his voice, "Sit here and close your eyes."

She obliged, waiting for the feeling of his lips against hers, but the kiss did not come.

Instead, a slurpy, wet tongue covered her face in saliva. It would have been gross; except she would recognize those licks anywhere. Her eyes flew open. "Wilson!" She shot a look at Ethan. "How did you— when did you—where was he—"

Ethan chuckled and patted the dog on the head. "Let's just say that I called in a favor with Nigel and urged him to ask for permission from the Maltenstein head of the household. He has an old schoolmate who works on their staff, and they arranged for Wilson to come along. So, Nigel and I smuggled him in. I know how stressed you've been about the games and the gala, and I wanted to offer some comfort. Your grandmother and Granny don't know he's here."

"Oh, boy. They'll be excited about this. Well, Granny will—she loves the drama. Grandmother—not so much." Claire scratched the top of her dog's head and then sent a grateful look to Ethan. "Thank you so much. This is exactly what I needed."

Ethan grinned. "I thought so, too. A smart queen told me once that petting a dog releases dopamine and lowers blood pressure, so I thought he might ease your anxiety—at least a little."

Chuckling, Claire leaned up and planted a soft kiss on her husband's lips. "Thank you." She yawned and stretched her arms overhead.

He raised a brow. "Tired?"

She nodded and covered her mouth as more yawns threatened to escape. "Exhausted."

He extended a hand to her. "Let's go to bed."

"Okay. You win." Rising from her seat with assistance from Ethan, she steadied herself once in a righted position. Claire held tight to Ethan's arm and followed him across the room and up the stairs. She had to trust that the Intercontinental Games and Fruhling Gala would go off without a hitch and everything would be brighter in the morning.

Wilson trailed behind them up the stairs and barked as if he agreed.

# Chapter 11

**Fraulein Halstaff stomped** about Claire's bedroom murmuring, "This will not do. It simply will not do." She scanned the pile of Claire's clothes lying rumpled in the middle of the bed and in a suitcase on the floor. "This is everything? What did I say? I told you to come prepared."

Claire glanced at the heap and shrugged. She recalled her conversation with Halstaff about her wardrobe and expectations as a fellow international host for the games. Still, Claire hadn't agreed with Halstaff's selections and had decided to coincidentally 'forget' a few items. Especially the black dress with the oversized fur hat that looked like she was wearing a blanket on her head. Not for her. Plus, it made Claire sneeze—she suspected she was allergic to the faux fur. "I don't know what to tell you. I brought everything that I thought I would need. I apologize if something was overlooked." *Like that hideous faux fur concoction.*

Fraulein Halstaff muttered something in

Maltensteinian and then pulled out a gown from the bottom of the stack after a few more minutes of digging. "Here. This will have to function. Not ideal." She said nothing more after that, spun on her heel, and exited the room.

She chuckled and stared at the dress in her hand. Somehow, Fraulein Halstaff had selected the most hideous dress Claire had brought. It figured. Oh, well. At least the weeks would pass, and then she'd go home and have a baby. She just had to make it through the games and the gala.

Someone rapped at the door.

Claire raised her head. "Come in."

Granny burst through and shuffled over to join Claire, already halfway through a conversation she'd likely been conducting with herself since ascending the stairs. "I know you don't like to hear this, but you must take a break. You can't—" She glanced at the dress in Claire's hand with a bodice of black velvet and a white lacy ruffle near the neck—reminiscent of an old-timey photo op at an amusement park. "What in the world is that thing?" Granny raised both brows.

Claire sent her granny a half-smile. "My wardrobe for the opening ceremony."

Granny pursed her lips together. "No. No way. You can't wear that thing. It's hideous. It's beyond hideous. It makes hideous look good."

Claire snorted. "Thanks. That makes me feel so much better." She tilted her head to the side, willing the gown to improve its appearance from a different angle. But alas, Granny was right. *Hideous*. "It's settled. I'm *not* wearing it." Claire tossed it back into the heap and turned to the opened suitcase with the rest of her garments. She rummaged through her belongings and pulled out an azure velvet gown.

Granny made a tsking sound. "Fraulein Halstaff isn't going to like that. It's not green, and she didn't approve it for today's event."

Claire and her granny locked eyes for a few seconds, and they both laughed. "It's never stopped us before. I'm wearing it, and I don't care what she says. Besides, I'll have on this heavy wool coat, so I doubt anyone will see my dress underneath."

Granny frowned. "Don't they usually take photographs right after the opening-ceremony speeches?"

The ceremony would take place outside, in the shadow of the biggest slope on the mountain. The thermometer outside read thirty degrees, but with the wind whipping hard, the air would feel much cooler. How long could they expect her to stand outside anyway? A few minutes? Not long enough for her to receive a lecture about her wardrobe. "It will be fine." With the final decision made, she slipped into the gown and pressed a rogue blonde tendril into place. After looking at her reflection in the mirror, she nodded, approving of the look. At least she felt more like herself in the sapphire blue—Amorley's color.

A knock sounded at the door, and Granny shuffled to answer it.

Nigel stood on the other side, shifted from foot to foot, and his cheeks flushed. He made grunting noises as he struggled with her dog in his arms.

"Nigel, you're going to hurt yourself. He weighs over eighty pounds. Put him down."

"Your Majesty, if I put him down, he will chew up the carpeting, steal your dress, run off with the dinner, or some other catastrophe. As you know, I'm quite fond of the guy, but he has been quite the headache today."

As if he understood that his behavior was being discussed, Wilson quit wrestling against Nigel and tucked his head under Nigel's chin.

"I'm sorry, Nigel. He'll do better. Should I take him with me?" Claire raised a brow.

Granny chimed in, "Not today. Let's get through one ceremony without someone choking on food, breaking a bone, or collapsing onto the floor. I love Wilson, too, but I don't think we need to add his mischief to the mix."

Claire turned her gaze to her sweet puppy dog, his eyes tempting her to cave and let him tag along, but she remained steadfast. "Sorry, buddy. Not today. But when I return, we'll snuggle. Promise."

He made a small whimper and resigned himself to his fate.

Nigel set him down, and Wilson trudged over to his fluffy bed in the corner of the room. After one circle on it, he nestled in and closed his eyes.

Claire smiled at her dog and longtime friend, "Believe me, if I could join you, I would." She hurried with a final swipe of lipstick and put in her drop earrings, completing the finishing touches. "Okay, I'm ready."

The two Thomson women took the stairs and exited the lodge to find another old-fashioned sleigh waiting for them.

Ethan had told her he would meet her at the slope as he had to call home and check on some family business.

Claire and her Granny slid into their seats and covered their laps with the green blankets provided. Drawing her white dress coat tighter, Granny still shivered. Claire had tried to convince her to stay back at the lodge because of the temperature, but Granny would hear nothing of it. A few minutes later, the sleigh stopped close to the site on the mountain where the opening ceremony would take place.

The two women exited the sleigh, and Claire joined her husband, the queen mother, and the Maltenstein royals at a makeshift stage in front of a ski lift.

Careful not to fall, she gripped the handrail tight and climbed the stairs to the stage. Taking her place near the front, she smiled at the gathering crowd and formally waved as her grandmother had taught her.

The queen of Maltenstein dipped her head toward

Claire, but her countenance remained stoic. "Your Majesty."

Claire debated whether to curtsy or bow in response to a fellow royal, but she opted for a similar head tip and replied with a simple, "Good day."

King Spickletz stepped up to the microphone stand and cleared his throat. He looked the part of a serious royal, wearing a hunter-green three-piece suit, complete with a bow tie and pocket square. Over his suit, a gray wool coat remained unbuttoned. Claire couldn't fathom how he withstood the weather. Her winter coat was buttoned up to her neck to the point she could hardly breathe, but at least it curtailed the blowing wind. Still, she shivered.

"Welcome to the Intercontinental Games. It is my pleasure to represent the great country of Maltenstein and co-host this event with the Amorley royal family. As you know, the Intercontinental Games represent the unity of humanity and allow us to compete in the spirit of peace and goodwill."

Claire forced herself not to roll her eyes. She hadn't seen much goodwill from the Maltensteins thus far. Granny's snort reached her ears from the audience. Scanning the crowd, Claire's eyes settled on the familiar face and searched for evidence of guilt.

Granny, to her credit, didn't falter but only sent Claire a small wink.

Claire smiled and turned her attention to the king of Maltenstein.

"The Intercontinental Games began decades ago and have continued every five years. As they have progressed since their beginning, the disciplines of bobsleigh, curling, cross-country skiing, skating, and downhill skiing have endured."

The crowd collectively nodded, waiting for him to wrap it up and start the games.

"As such, it is my pleasure to turn over the remainder of the opening remarks to the…lovely Dr. Claire Thomson, Queen of Amorley."

The crowd applauded, and Claire exhaled the breath she'd been holding since he paused as if searching for the best descriptor for her. At least he hadn't landed on an offensive one. He could have chosen so many other words.

Claire moved forward, ready to take her place at a second microphone set up about five feet from King Spickletz. She gasped as soon as her black-heeled booted foot took the first step. *Oh no*. Her right foot slid up in the air, and her left followed. She was going down. Hard.

Everything happened in slow motion. One moment her body hung in limbo horizontally, and then the next second, she hit the ground with a painful thud. The force of the fall knocked the wind out of her, and she struggled to regain her breath. Once the initial shock of the tumble had passed, Claire winced, rubbing her side. She'd have a bruise. Thankfully, she'd not hit her head and, as she wiggled her fingers and toes, didn't discern any broken bones—something for which to be thankful.

Ethan rushed to her side and sank next to her. He frowned, concern clouding his eyes. "Are you all right?"

She raised herself onto one elbow and surveyed her body again before answering, "I think so. I'll be sore tomorrow, though."

He reached under her arm, supporting her into an upright position. "Maybe you should stay still and let me call an ambulance."

Claire looked into the crowd and noticed the wide eyes and gaping jaws. So much for propriety and grace. She smiled at the crowd and gave them another formal wave. *Too little too late.* "No, I have to give this speech."

Ethan frowned. "At least promise me you'll let the doctor check you and the baby afterward."

Flashbulbs began throughout the crowd and lit up the space like lights on a Christmas tree.

*Super.* She glanced at her sweet husband again. "I promise." She still didn't know how she'd fallen—not that she wasn't awkward at times, but she hadn't seen this stumble coming. As she struggled to her feet, the ground felt really slick. Claire leaned over to Ethan. "Is the entire stage an ice rink? Is it just me? Is it my shoes?"

Ethan's eyes darted down to the stage floor and traced a small arc with his dress shoe. "No, it's icy. The rest of the stage isn't like this." He let go of her after he'd ensured she could stand still for a moment and took a few steps across to the other side of the stage before returning to her side. "Something's not right with this section of the stage. It's almost as if someone coated it in water and let it freeze."

Claire narrowed her eyes and flicked her gaze toward the Maltenstein faction. The wife looked particularly pleased with herself. She smirked and then turned around as if in a deep conversation with Fraulein Halstaff, who stood next to her.

Claire whispered into Ethan's ear, "I bet the Maltensteins did it. Maybe it was the queen. I don't know, but I'm sure someone in the Maltenstein camp had a part to play in this. They don't want us to succeed this week and would love to make me look bad."

Ethan lowered his voice, "I think you're right. How far will they go to promote their country and its interests?"

Claire didn't have time to consider this point but filed that tidbit away to mull over later. "I don't know, but I must say something right now to salvage this fiasco." She glanced at the microphone just beyond the impromptu ice rink. "Ethan, can you bring the microphone over here?"

He nodded and carefully retrieved the microphone, taking short, steady steps on his way back to where his wife stood. "Here you go."

Claire hoisted herself straighter and steadied herself against the microphone stand. Glancing at her husband, she sent him a grateful smile. "Thank you." Then, she turned toward the audience. "Please excuse my clumsiness. It appears that the slopes aren't the only icy thing around here. The slick ground by the podium caused me to tumble, but I'm all right."

Murmurs filled the crowd, but concerned frowns transformed into encouraging smiles.

"Right. Back to the matter at hand—the Intercontinental Games to be followed by the Fruhling Gala. As Amorley's representative, it thrills me to share this spectacular event with you. I pray that the following weeks will build a bridge of unity between our nations, and we will inspire one another toward greatness.

"Today's first event will be the bobsleigh. As the teams take the course, I encourage everyone to participate in patriotism with respect and honor. Without further delay, let the games begin. Thank you." Claire stepped away from the microphone and allowed Ethan to guide her off the stage, supporting her elbow. Her backside and spine throbbed, but at least everything still worked. It could have been worse.

The queen of Maltenstein, lips pursed, approached Claire as she exited the stage. "Such a pity to take a spill like that. You should be more careful with your steps—you could have been severely injured."

Claire scanned the woman's face to search for genuine concern. Something about how the woman spoke reminded Claire of her stepmother, Maurelle.

Tilting her head, Claire paused before responding, "I'll keep that in mind for the future. Hopefully, there won't be the need for such care, as I would not expect the stage or any other surface to be an issue moving forward. I will chat with the head of operations for the Intercontinental Games and my staff as they prepare for the Fruhling Gala to ensure nothing treacherous occurs from this point on."

The woman crossed her arms in front of her chest and sent Claire a half-smile. "See that you do." Then, she turned and sauntered away, rejoining her Maltenstein crew.

Claire and Ethan made their way to an awaiting sleigh.

Granny had already taken her seat in the sleigh and tucked her blanket across her lap. She leaned closer to Claire. "I don't like that Maltenstein woman. If I didn't know better, I'd think she was related to old Maurelle. They both send a shiver down my spine with the same ease. Must be a skill or something."

That nugget from her Granny evoked a shiver somewhere in her torso, but before she had time to reflect on it further, Dr. Brickworth appeared at the side of the sleigh. She wore a long red coat that matched her hair and enhanced her emerald eyes, though they crinkled with concern. "I saw that fall. I'm worried."

Claire waved away the fuss. "I'm sure that I'm fine. Nothing broken." She gestured a at her legs with her hands. "See? Good as new."

The obstetrician stared at Claire for a minute as if considering her options but then shook her head. "I don't care how fine you feel now. You need to go directly back to the lodge and lie down. I'm bringing over a portable ultrasound machine and checking your vitals. You're too close to your delivery date, and I don't want to take any chances."

Claire sighed. "Okay. You win. I'll let you check me over."

The entire crew prepared themselves for the frigid trek to the lodge, and Claire tried to ignore the tinge of pain growing in her low back. Maybe it wouldn't hurt to let Dr. Brickworth take a look at her.

# Chapter 12

Ethan had never seen Claire so angry. He rubbed her shoulders, trying to soothe her. "It's only for the week. Besides, it's like walking through an iceberg out there. The rest of us will be jealous. You get to stay inside where it's warm," he joked, attempting to cheer up his wife.

"I don't want to be warm and comfortable. I want to serve my country and represent them to the best of my ability. This—" she swept her hands across the bed—"is not the best of my ability."

"You have to take care of yourself—and the baby. It's for the best right now." He took her hand in his and leaned closer. Brushing a strand of hair from her face, Ethan pressed his lips against her forehead, each cheek, and then her lips.

His heart pounded as he inhaled the scent of her lavender perfume. Even after getting married and carrying the weight of guiding a country, Claire still made his palms sweat and his pulse quicken. Her golden locks and clear blue eyes made her a breathtaking woman, but she remained one of the kindest people he'd known. She was a beautiful soul.

Raising his head, Ethan whispered, "I love you. Things will look better after some rest. I promise."

Claire screwed up her face in childish disgust and stuck out her tongue.

"Lovely." Ethan chuckled.

"Fine." She sighed. "I give up. I'll stay in bed for now, but I'm not missing the downhill skiing event, the closing ceremony, or the Fruhling Gala. Even if you must carry me there, push me in a sleigh, or heave me on a gurney. I'm going."

Ethan raised his hands in defeat. "All right. If the doctor clears you to attend those events, I'll support you."

The corners of Claire's lips lifted into a bright smile. "Good. Now, you'd better go. We can't have the world seeing only the Maltenstein leaders on television and in the newspapers. *You* have to represent the country."

Ethan saluted her and snapped his feet to attention. "Yes, Your Majesty."

Claire rolled her eyes and pulled her blanket closer to her chin. She yawned and closed her eyes. Her back still ached. Fortunately, Dr. Brickworth had only diagnosed her with a muscle strain but insisted she take it easy for a week. "Maybe a short nap wouldn't be the worst thing in the world."

Gratitude for his wife filled his heart. "No, maybe

not. Get some rest, my love." Then, he turned to leave the room, determined to stand his ground against any attack on his country, his family, and his future. No matter what it took, he'd ensure that Amorley and Claire's legacy survived. It was for the good of his people. Ethan believed God had ordained her for a time such as this. He wouldn't let the Maltenstein leaders, Maurelle, Fraulein Halstaff, or anyone else get in the way.

# Chapter 13

**The week passed** in slow motion. Claire remained in bed, continuing her role as the dutiful patient to the best of her ability—and by that, she meant that she'd only been yelled at for getting out of bed three times when she had an irresistible craving for donuts and snuck down to the kitchen to find some.

The queen mother had given her a stern lecture on bedrest and the importance of a balanced diet.

Claire laughed as she recalled the conversation. She sat up in bed and stretched her arms overhead, yawning. The day had come—the Intercontinental Games pinnacle event—the downhill ski. Hundreds of thousands of fans would attend, and all major-media outlets—television stations, news syndicates, and many celebrities had confirmed their reservations.

Claire jumped out of bed as fast as her burgeoning baby bump would allow and contorted herself into the sapphire gown Fraulein Halstaff had selected for her. Standing in front of the mirror in her room, Claire let her eyes scan her ensemble. Large diamond-drop earrings hung from her ears, and one of Fraulein Halstaff's minions had swept Claire's blonde locks into an elegant, if not painfully tight, chignon. *Not bad.* Despite Fraulein Halstaff's record of possibly trying to destroy Amorley and Claire's legacy, the woman had given Claire a fashionable look.

*God, please let today go well.* Things had gone from one disaster to another, and today had to be a success.

Wilson scooted over to Claire's side and butted his nose against her hand, insisting that she give him attention.

Petting his head, she smiled down at him. "I don't know if I can take you with me today, buddy. You don't have the best track record for good behavior at important events." He settled his sweet chocolate brown eyes on her and sat his rear down—the picture of obedience. His pleading look tugged at her heart, and her resolve weakened. "Okay, you may come along, but you must stay with Nigel at the sleigh. You can't come anywhere near the stage. If today doesn't go well, my grandmother will flip out, and the Maltenstein rulers will use it as more ammunition against us. I don't know their angle, but I don't trust them. They want to make Amorley or me look bad; I can't let that happen. Understand?" She raised her brow.

The dog tilted his head and opened his mouth, panting. He smiled, so Claire took that to mean he understood. She shook her head and shrugged on her coat, hat, and gloves. "All right, come on." Claire waved for him to follow her outside to their awaiting ride. Opening the door, a cold blast of wind hit Claire's face. "Ugh."

Ethan joined her at the front door and rubbed her shoulders. "It still feels like the arctic circle, doesn't it?"

With chattering teeth, Claire nodded. "More like frozen tundra. Solid ice." Her eyes drifted to the vehicle waiting to carry them to the skiing event. *Another sleigh.* She sighed.

The sleigh held a mound of luggage. Claire arched a brow and turned to Ethan. "What's all that?" She pointed toward the stack of bags.

Ethan frowned. "That is your grandmother and Fraulein Halstaff's doing. Apparently, we have to change into different clothes for the closing ceremony and again for a meet and greet with the press afterward. Shaking his head, Ethan helped Claire into the sleigh and then sat beside her. The rest of her party loaded into other sleighs behind them, and they took off toward the ski lift.

They had almost arrived at the mountain's pinnacle when the sleigh hit a hidden mound of snow. The sudden bump in the path jarred the sleigh and its occupants with an abrupt jolt, and Claire reached out for Ethan's arm to steady herself.

Ethan turned his gaze upon his bride. "Are you all right?"

Claire nodded. "It wasn't that hard of a jolt. It just took me by surprise. You can't expect a completely uneventful trek across a mountain on a sleigh." The words had barely escaped her lips when the force of another bump dislodged a small piece of luggage, and Claire watched as it rolled down the hillside.

Unfortunately, that one small suitcase must have supported the entire mound because as the little brown rectangle flipped and scooted down the mountain, the rest of the pile of luggage followed, resembling pieces of sand slipping through an hourglass.

Claire's hand flew to her mouth. "Oh my! We have to do something."

Wilson took this as his cue to jump into action. He lunged out the side of the still-moving sleigh and bounded down the hillside, his legs kicking up a flurry of snow behind him.

"Stop the sleigh!" Ethan shouted to the driver. Claire and Ethan grabbed the seatback in front of them to brace themselves for the stop. The sleigh came to an abrupt halt.

Claire glanced over her shoulder, and her eyes landed on her rambunctious dog.

Wilson grabbed one of the smaller pieces of luggage in his mouth and shook it furiously. This effort tore open the bag, and its contents dotted the pristine white snowscape with most of Claire's ensembles for the rest of the day. He rooted around through his prizes, probably sniffing for Claire's scent. His teeth clamped onto a black dress, he turned around and hurried back toward Claire's sleigh, a victorious sparkle in his dark eyes.

"Oh no," Claire whispered.

Ethan raked his fingers through his hair. "Your grandmother is going to have his head."

Claire put her hand to her forehead. "Forget about my grandmother. Fraulein Halstaff, and the Maltenstein crew will not let this go. They'll use it against me. I don't care about the dress or the other things, but this will end up in the press tomorrow, if not sooner."

Her misbehaving dog arrived at the side of the sleigh and jumped up, resting his paws on the seat. He dropped the dress in her lap, looking pleased with himself with his tongue hanging out the side of his mouth.

Claire couldn't help but love the furry rascal. Scratching his head, she leaned closer. "You are such a little scamp. I know you're a retriever, but couldn't you leave well enough alone just once?"

The dog continued panting and tilted his head. He must have sensed Claire's reproach because he leaned closer and slurped her face with his wet tongue.

Claire giggled until the queen mother and Fraulein Halstaff sidled next to the sleigh.

Fraulein Halstaff crossed her arms in front of her chest. "What is the meaning of this? Must you insist on ruining every event with that wretched canine?"

Claire opened her mouth to explain, but the queen

mother chimed in, "Really, Claire, I have told you to leave Wilson at home for important events because, sadly, he cannot be trusted. I know he is dear to you, but unfortunately, we have an image to uphold and responsibilities to tend to, and we cannot meet our obligations if he runs down a mountainside and causes our luggage to spill."

"But he didn't do it. Yes, he chased the luggage down the mountain, but he didn't cause the spill. We hit a bump and then—"

Fraulein Halstaff raised her hand, interrupting, "There's no time for this discussion. We are already late for the downhill-skiing event. I will have my staff clean up your mess again, and we will continue on our way to avoid a further delay in the games."

Claire shivered. "Fine." She feared she'd regret saying anything further on the matter—not that Fraulein Halstaff would let her get a word in.

The Maltenstein crew barked orders to their staff, and a flurry of minions jumped into action cleaning up the spill.

Fraulein Halstaff and the Maltenstein rulers returned to their sleighs, as did the queen mother.

Wilson jumped over the side of Claire's sleigh and curled up at her feet as if nothing had gone amiss. She rubbed his head one last time. "Honestly, just one day. Please behave for one day."

A sigh slipped from the pup's mouth, and he nestled further and closed his eyes.

"Right." She glanced at Ethan. "We'd better hurry since we're so late."

Ethan spoke to the driver and then sat back in his seat, tucking the blanket around his wife.

Countless minutes later, they arrived at the location of the downhill-skiing event. The wind whipped at Claire's whole body, piercing the multiple layers of warmth she'd donned for the day. She shivered and focused on the scenery. The sun shone overhead, and the light rays glinted off the snow, casting diamonds across the landscape.

Ethan helped her exit the sleigh, and Wilson followed behind.

"Wow." She smiled at Ethan, forgetting the chaos from earlier for a moment. "It's beautiful up here."

He took her hand in his. "It is. Especially now that you're here."

She laughed and ribbed him in the side. "So cheesy, but I love you, too."

When Granny and the queen mother exited their rides and took their places at Claire's side, the Intercontinental Games president approached her group and led them toward the main stage. Claire, Ethan, the queen mother, Granny, Wilson, and the Maltenstein faction followed him with their security team in tow.

Claire grasped the handrail leading up the stairs to the main stage. She glanced at Ethan, who stood a step behind her. "I'm not falling today. More bed rest does not sound appealing to me."

He grinned and rested a hand on her back, giving her extra support. Leaning close, he whispered in her ear, "I won't let you fall again."

The sound and texture of his voice sent a tingle down her spine. Her heartbeat quickened, and her cheeks warmed. She loved this man. Even though they were married and expecting a child, he made her heart soar just as much as when they first met.

Claire glanced at the crowd in attendance, raising her hand to shield her eyes from the blinding sunlight.

A figure dressed in a long black coat with a hood moved in the back of the crowd, catching Claire's attention. She squinted, trying to make out the person's face, but she couldn't identify the mystery person due to the distance between them and the sun's brightness.

The shrouded figure crossed to the other side and, at some point, became lost in the crowd, but something about how the woman moved triggered a spark of familiarity in Claire's mind. Once her eyes had lost the trail of the shrouded person, Claire turned her attention to the task at hand. Even so, a needling concern tugged at her brain. *Who was that hooded figure, and where had she seen her before?*

Wilson somehow slipped from Ethan's grasp and jogged up next to Claire, almost as if he intended to protect her. He sat down next to her in an uncharacteristically calm manner and let out a low growl. The dog didn't like something or someone at the event.

She peered down at him and whispered, "It's okay. Behave. I'm fine."

Claire didn't get a chance to answer her questions about the mystery woman or console Wilson because the Intercontinental Games president nodded at her, indicating for her to take her place at the microphone.

Claire stepped forward and cleared her throat. "Welcome to the final Intercontinental Games event. It has been my pleasure to witness, albeit from my bed while watching on the television this week—"

The crowd chuckled.

"—all the wonderful displays of athleticism and patriotism at the games. Thank you to every participant, sponsor, and fellow Amorley citizen who participated in this year's Intercontinental Games. I hope and pray that this will solidify a bond of unity between our countries and improve open relationships for years to come."

*Yeah, right.* Not likely when the Maltenstein crew seemed to have it out for her, but Claire couldn't say that to the crowd, and honestly, it *was* her hope that things would improve. So, she hadn't told a lie. "This brings me to the reason we all stand here today. The downhill-skiing race will conclude these games, and as the teams are tied in medals, this race will represent a tiebreaker."

The race official joined Claire at her side. He dipped his head in her direction. "Your Majesty," he acknowledged, and she handed the microphone to him.

She sent him a smile. "Thank you."

The man raised the microphone closer to his mouth. "Are the racers ready?" He paused, waiting for any objections from the racers or their handlers. Receiving none, he continued, "If not, then we will begin on my count. On your mark, get set, and…go."

Another gentleman fired a shot in the air overhead to signify the start of the race, and the racers blazed down the hill. Snow kicked up on either side of each participant as they cut snaking paths down the mountain.

At first, one of the Amorley competitors held a strong lead, and Claire's fellow citizens shouted and cheered in the crowd. It looked like he would take the win, tipping Amorley ahead in the medal count and securing bragging rights for her country. Not to mention it wouldn't hurt her credibility as queen to have ruled over a winning Intercontinental Games season. She would take all the help in that department she could get.

Out of nowhere, the black figure Claire had seen earlier emerged from the edge of the crowd and raced toward the racers.

Wilson growled again, this time louder, and started barking.

Claire lunged for her dog. "No, Wilson, wait. Don't." Before she could calm him down, he shot off at full speed. His legs pumped furiously, flinging white powder around him like a snow globe.

Total mayhem ensued.

Wilson stampeded through the downhill race, determined to catch the mystery person in black. Several skiers dodged him as he crossed the middle of the course.

Claire held her breath, praying that no one would hit him. It looked like he had made it through unscathed, but as she released the air from her lungs, the final skier from Maltenstein plowed into Wilson.

Claire gasped. Both hands flew to her mouth. *No.* She took off as fast as her legs would allow and hurried down the stairs and across the snowy mountain to where the skier had collided with her dog.

The man lay on the ground, clutching his knee while Wilson remained on his side nearby.

Ethan came behind Claire a few seconds later, winded. He furrowed his brow. "What can I do?"

She flicked her eyes toward him for a brief moment. "Call 911—or whatever they have here. Get a medic, an ambulance, a snowmobile—something. I'll do what I can for the racer. Can you check on Wilson?"

Ethan nodded and hurried away to call for help.

Tears stung her eyes. Why did bad things keep happening to her? Even though she messed up, she tried to do the right thing.

The verse from Joshua 1:9 circled her thoughts. "Have I not commanded you? Be strong and courageous. Do not be afraid; do not be discouraged, for the Lord your God will be with you wherever you go."

*Don't be afraid. Pull it together, Claire. God will help.* Easier said than believed sometimes.

She caught the skier's eyes. "What hurts?"

He groaned and clutched his right knee. His goggles had gotten twisted and sat askew on his face. It looked like he had a black eye forming, but thankfully he'd been wearing a helmet.

Claire frowned. "Try not to move. I need to check your neck and back to ensure you didn't damage your spine, and then I'll look at your leg. Okay?"

He grimaced and whispered, "Fine."

She scooted closer to his head and palpated down his spine, ensuring she couldn't find any inconsistencies. Once she'd cleared his neck and back, she checked the motor function of his extremities. "Can you wiggle your fingers and move your feet?" she asked.

He obliged but grimaced. "My knee feels like it is out of joint." He groaned once more.

She sent him an empathetic smile and turned her attention to his area of concern. "Your spine looks good. I don't think you've had a concussion, and there doesn't seem to be any damage to your neck or back, so that's good. Let me see about your leg."

Claire placed her hands gently on his right knee and caught his gaze. "May I?"

He nodded and remained rigid.

She maneuvered his knee in several different

directions, tugging and pushing to assess the intactness of his ligaments and joints. He groaned and grimaced throughout the exam but let her complete it.

She released his knee and sat back. "You tore your MCL."

He grabbed his leg again. "My MC, what?"

She nodded. "Your medial collateral ligament. You tore it when you fell. We won't know for sure until we get you to the hospital and I order an MRI, but I've been doing this for a long time. It's torn. I'm so sorry."

While she'd examined the injured skier, Ethan had retrieved help and returned to tend to Wilson.

Claire glanced over, noted that Wilson had roused, and stood up. He tossed his head and knocked the snow off himself with a full-body shake. A second or two later, he wagged his tail and looked like nothing had gone awry.

Ethan caught her gaze. "I think he'll live." He chuckled and then glanced at the skier. "How's our other patient?"

"He'll be all right, too." Claire waved over the two medics who had arrived on a snowmobile and explained the situation to them, "He needs to be taken to the closest hospital and have an MRI done. I'd recommend a head CT, too, although his mental status is intact, and it doesn't look like he suffered a concussion. His c-spine is clear, too."

The medics jumped into action and transferred the patient from the snowy ground onto a snow toboggan stretcher, securing him with straps and a blanket. They carried the stretcher to the snowmobile and attached it to the back of it.

Snow began to fall, creating a thin layer of confetti across the toboggan.

The ski patrol left, carrying the injured skier on the red toboggan behind them. Only then did Claire release a sigh. A twinge of pain caught her side, and her hand flew to her abdomen. Doubling over, she groaned.

Ethan quickly placed a hand around her to steady her. "What's wrong? What happened?"

Claire's lower abdomen tensed, and the cramping pain took her breath away. She couldn't answer for a few seconds. As the wave of agony subsided, she slowly straightened. Sweat beaded across her forehead, and nausea swept over her. "Um—uh—it's, it's a cramp. Probably dehydrated, or I overexerted myself. That's all it is. I—agh!" she screamed and doubled over again.

Ethan rubbed her back with his hand. "That's it. I'm sending for the ski patrol again. You need an examination."

Claire shook her head, placing one hand on her thigh and bracing herself while signaling for him to give her a minute with her other hand. After a few more seconds, she righted herself again. "I'm not going to the hospital. It's probably Braxton-Hicks contractions."

Ethan raised a brow. "False labor?"

"Yeah, it happens all the time. I didn't drink

enough water today, and then we had all that excitement on the way up here, and then the skier got hurt, and I overdid it. That's all. I'm positive. Besides, I must see the race through and make closing remarks."

As Claire rubbed her abdomen and pulled in another breath, a tall figure approached her. Seeing the person's face proved hard until he came close to her. One of the Intercontinental Games officials she recognized from earlier gave a respectful bow.

"Your Majesty, we've concluded the race and designated a winner because a snow squall has hit us. We all need to seek shelter. The racers at the bottom of the course are being transported to the main lodge. Not many of us are still here. When the skier got injured, the ski patrol ordered us to clear the hill because of the approaching storm. The only ones remaining are us, your grandmother, the woman calling herself Granny, and your dog."

Claire turned to Ethan. "What are we going to do? We can't make it down the mountain now."

The official stepped closer. "If I may make a suggestion—a smaller lodge nearby is often used for visiting dignitaries and other guests. At the moment, it's empty. We can go there for shelter. Usually, these storms blow over quickly."

Claire caught Ethan's gaze. "My contractions stopped for now. I don't see that we have much of a choice. What do you think?"

The snow fell harder, obscuring more than a

hand's length in front of them. "I think it's our best option."

The remaining group trudged through the rising snow to the nearby cabin. They arrived at a beautiful, quaint structure, albeit a bit rustic. The cabin had a wooden exterior and a ceiling with a snow-blanketed roof.

Ethan pushed through the powder covering the front porch and checked the door handle. "It's locked."

The games' official moved past him. "Here, I have keys to all the buildings that are part of the facilities." He put it in the lock and turned, then squeezed the door handle, and it gave way. Stepping aside, he turned to the shivering group. "After you, Your Majesty."

Sliding past the gentleman, Claire sent him a smile. "Thank you." She entered the main room and noted a stone-faced fireplace on one side and a small kitchen on the other. A staircase at the back of the room traversed to a second level. The room still held a chill, but at least it was protected from the wind and blinding snowfall and promised a warm fire to come.

"This is perfect." She turned to face the official. "Thank you for thinking of this place. I don't know how we would have reached the main lodge." She absentmindedly rubbed her abdomen, and her shoulders relaxed. At least her contractions had stopped for now.

Ethan stepped closer. His brow furrowed. "Is everything all right? Are you in pain?"

She shook her head and took his hand, giving it a

squeeze. "I'm fine."

Nigel approached the couple. "Would you like me to start a fire?"

Claire removed her coat, and Nigel took it from her. She thanked him, shook off the snow from her hair, and stepped out of her wet shoes. "That would be wonderful. How long do you think the storm will last?"

He draped her coat over his arm. "Hopefully, a few hours at the most if it is a true snow squall."

Claire's shoulders relaxed. "That's good. Let's hope for that."

Nigel bowed and then carried her coat over to a small closet. He hung up all the jackets and then shut the door. Afterward, he turned his attention to the empty fireplace, stacking a series of logs in the middle and lighting the kindling.

About twenty minutes later, a roaring blaze filled the room with heat.

Claire had finally stopped shivering and settled on the couch with a blanket and cup of tea that Nigel had made.

The queen mother and Granny joined her in two oversized chairs.

Ethan settled next to her and accepted another mug from Nigel. "Thank you." He took a sip and sank back against the couch, resting his hand behind Claire's shoulder. Pulling her closer, he planted a quick kiss on her head. "I love you."

She tilted her head up and smiled at him. "I love

you, too." For at least an hour, Claire sat next to Ethan, chatting with her granny and grandmother. She enjoyed the warmth of her family and safe shelter.

Fortunately, Wilson had behaved since their arrival and stayed curled up on a rug in front of the fireplace. His eyes were closed, but he twitched a leg every now and then as if he were having the best dream. Perhaps he was chasing another rogue suitcase down a mountain.

Glancing out the window, Claire tensed. "It's still snowing—a lot. What if we get stuck here for days?" A brief concern about her due date flashed through her mind.

"I'm certain we can get down the mountain before that happens." Ethan gave her a squeeze.

She stared into his brilliant blue eyes. Claire could get lost in them for hours. Something about looking into them made her feel at home. Her shoulders relaxed a bit more as her thoughts shifted toward the future and the hope of a new family and putting past hurts behind her. Life would be good. "You're right. I'm sure you're right. Besides, my due date isn't for several more weeks, and it's my first baby, so it's doubtful that I'll go into early labor with my first pregnancy." She repeated this information in her mind to reassure herself.

He sent her a warm smile. "Exactly."

The wind whistled outside and picked up in intensity, causing the sides of the house to creak and the roof to shake. Ethan peered up. "Yikes. That doesn't sound promising."

Nigel moved closer to the window and peered outside.

Suddenly, a loud crack sounded, and then a thud shook the cabin with a force so great that Claire suspected the structure would split in two.

The power went out, and the sound of the humming of the furnace and the refrigerator ceased. All the lights in the room faded to black, and the only glow filling the space emanated from the fireplace.

Granny's eyes widened. "What in the name of all things good was that?"

Ethan had paled but, to his credit, he remained calm. "Probably just a branch fell on the roof or side of the house and knocked out the power. It usually sounds much worse than it is." He rose from the couch and crossed the room to the closet where Nigel had hung his coat. He opened it and pulled out his outerwear, shrugging into the jacket and donning his boots.

Claire turned and rested her chin on the back of the sofa. "What are you doing?"

He tugged on his gloves and hat. "I'll go see what happened. Perhaps I can move whatever fell out of the way. I'll be back quickly."

Worry pulled at Claire's heart, but how much trouble could Ethan get into outside the cabin? "Okay but be careful."

He nodded, opened the door, and a blast of cold

wind and snow filled the main room. As he stepped out the door, Wilson darted from his resting state as if nudged by a hot poker. He zipped ahead of Ethan. "I guess he's coming with me to help," he said over his shoulder and chuckled.

Claire sent him a nervous grin. "I guess so. Look out for one another."

He waved his gloved hand at her, then nodded. Shutting the door behind him with a thud, the sound echoed around the room. It carried a finality that caused Claire to shiver from more than the cold—she had a terrible feeling about all of this.

# Chapter 14

Trudging through the snow that covered the height of his boots, Ethan felt his legs and feet filled with icy sludge grow numb. He pulled the hood on his coat over his tobogganed head and prayed for the precipitation and wind to cease.

Darkness had settled around the landscape in the short time since they'd arrived at the cabin, but unfortunately, the storm didn't show any sign of weakening. Snowflakes pelted his cheeks like miniature sharp swords, and he could hardly see to walk more than a step in front of him.

Wilson had vanished around the corner of the cabin—at least, he hoped that's where the pup had gone.

As Ethan turned the corner to where the power source should be, his eyes scanned for the beloved family dog.

No Wilson.

"Wilson? Come here, boy. Wilson," he shouted a few times.

The barking sounded distant but grew louder as Claire's furry friend approached. He stopped short of knocking Ethan to the ground and wagged his tail, happy to be outside.

Ethan scratched the dog's head. "You think this is fun, don't you?"

Wilson seemed to smile, his tongue hanging out to one side, the dog oblivious to the stressful situation.

As he looked for the power source, Ethan talked out loud to Wilson to keep himself focused and calm, then he got to work, "Let's see. I'd guess the power box would be right here—ah, here it is."

He hunched down to inspect the unit that had fallen to the ground and a large piece of a tree branch that sat beside it. He looked up toward the roofline and noted the giant branch responsible for the thunderous sound earlier. Now it sprawled across the roof. He glanced at the dog. "I guess we should give thanks that it didn't split the house down the middle. That branch is rather large." He stared at the damaged power box and then turned to Wilson again. "It doesn't look good. We won't be repairing it tonight, I'm afraid."

When a finger tapped him on the shoulder, he whipped around so fast that he nearly whacked the interloper in the face.

Nigel stood before him, bundled from head to toe.

Ethan exhaled a sigh of relief. "You can't do that. You startled me."

"Sir." His face paled.

Ethan's stomach plummeted. "What? What happened?"

Nigel wrung his hands. "It's Her Majesty."

Shooting straight upright, Ethan held his breath as his gut turned to ice. After two seconds of processing Nigel's words, Ethan darted toward the cabin and blasted through the door. "What's going on? Are you all right? Is it the baby?"

Claire stood draped over the back of the couch, holding the frame with both hands. She grunted between bated breaths, "I—think—I'm—in—labor." A guttural yelp escaped her lips and echoed throughout the dimly lit room.

What would he do? They couldn't blindly walk down the mountain at this hour, with the wind still howling and snow blinding their eyes. They had no transportation to reach the hospital safely. The phones and Wi-Fi remained nonfunctional, so calling for help was not an option. He turned to face Nigel, who'd followed behind him and had just come in the door, huffing and puffing from exertion. "What do we do now? She can't have the baby here."

Granny, who'd changed into her usual monochromatic tracksuit, this time in a blinding orange shade that matched her hair color, sidled up next to Ethan and whispered, "We may not have much of a choice. Her contractions are two minutes apart and last at least a minute each time. I'm not a doctor, but that sounds like things are moving along, and the baby will be here before you get her out of here.”

Ethan lowered his voice, “Two minutes?”

She pursed her lips and fiddled with the gold chain ball necklace she always wore. “Yep. Afraid so.”

Claire moaned again. “I—can—hear—you. Also, I’m—a—doctor.” She stopped and held one finger in the air—her signal for a moment to regroup before continuing her conversation.

About thirty seconds passed, and Granny joined her granddaughter’s side, rubbing her back and trying to comfort her.

The queen mother paced in front of the fireplace.

Finally, Claire righted herself. “Okay. That one’s over.” She caught Ethan’s gaze. “She’s right. I’m progressing too fast to go anywhere else. Go boil some water for sterilizing. We don’t have long to—.” After another painful contraction subsided, Claire stretched her back and let her granny swipe her forehead with a damp washcloth. Claire glanced at her family and staff. “Find some fitted and regular sheets. Towels, washcloths. A blanket or two.” She blew out a breath. “See if the bathroom has medical supplies. Rubbing alcohol, gauze, a thermometer.” She winced. “Also, find candles and flashlights.” She took a shaky breath. “Check the kitchen drawers. See if you can find bowls and trash bags.”

Everyone jumped into action, scattering to retrieve whatever Claire needed.

Granny tracked down a bathrobe that hung in one

of the bathrooms and convinced Claire to change into it under the guise that it would make delivery easier while maintaining some degree of modesty. She helped Claire into the bedroom.

Ethan continued calling for help on his cell phone as he looked for extra candles and flashlights and gave the fire some tending to so it didn't die. Claire had taken residence on the bed and was lying on her side when Ethan entered the bedroom and settled beside her on the floor, taking her hand in his. "It's going to be all right. I promise I won't let anything happen to you." He closed his eyes and lifted up a short prayer for protection and blessing through their difficult situation. When he opened his eyes, tears ran down Claire's cheeks.

"I'm sorry about all of this," she said as he wiped away a tear with his thumb. Claire shook her head. "I don't mean to complain. We're so blessed, but this isn't how I intended for any of this to go. I'm supposed to deliver in my hospital, hooked up to a monitor, safe and warm. Not trapped in a remote cabin in the middle of a snowstorm."

Ethan brought her hand to his lips, kissed it, and stared into her eyes. "I know. But I know that God has a plan and will always work things out for our good, even the bad things. We have to trust Him."

Claire squeezed his hand—hard.

"Bad one?" he asked.

She closed her eyes and winced. A few seconds

later, she expelled the breath she'd been holding and uttered a short, "Yep."

A knock at the door interrupted, and Ethan called, "Come in."

Granny entered the room and sat on the bed near Claire's feet. "How are things coming along?"

Claire released Ethan's hand and pushed herself into a half-sitting position with her back resting against a mound of pillows. She tucked the top of her robe tighter. "It feels like I have to push. I don't know how I know that, but that's exactly what it feels like."

Granny made a tsking sound. "Then, you have to push. That's how you know it's time."

Ethan shot Granny a glance. "What should I do?"

Granny pulled the blankets down to the bottom of the bed and scooted closer to her granddaughter. She peered at Ethan. "You're not going to faint on me, are you?"

He swallowed hard. "No," he whispered. At least, he hoped not. He had to be strong for Claire.

Granny gave a firm nod. "Good. Then, tell everyone outside to give us some privacy unless they hear us yelling for help, and see if they can get the phone to work. Otherwise, we're having a baby."

Ethan ran out of the room and relayed Granny's orders, focusing on taking slow, steady breaths before he returned to the room. They were having a baby—he and Claire. They were going to become parents. Today. A slow smile tugged at the corners of his mouth. In a few short hours, he'd be a father. As scary as the day had been, that thought filled his heart with happiness and hope. Nothing would go wrong.

# Chapter 15

Claire gazed down at the baby in her arms. *I'm a mom. How weird.* In one moment, her entire life had changed. The experience both thrilled and terrified her.

Granny scooted closer to Claire and held her arms out. "Give her here. I need to hold my great-granddaughter. Seeing as I helped bring her into this world, I get to hold her next."

Ethan chuckled. He'd already held his daughter and peppered her forehead and cheeks with kisses. Claire found it sweet to see. The look of relief painted across his face that both mother and baby had safely made it through the birth pleased Claire. She felt thankful—things could have gone badly in this remote location, but God had given them an uneventful labor and delivery.

Claire handed the baby to her granny and watched as the woman who'd helped raise her took the bundle of joy into her arms and cooed at her sweet face. Granny glanced over at Claire.

Granny studied the little girl's face, and her voice

softened, "She looks like your mother. That would've pleased Mona." She touched the baby's cheek. "I wish your grandmother could have met you. She would have been over the moon."

Tears filled Claire's eyes, and her throat ached. "I wish she could be here, too."

Granny kissed the baby's head. "What's the final decision on her name? Will she take after good ole granny and be called Margaret?"

"Actually," Claire took Ethan's hand, "we decided to call her Rosemarie Mona Kane. I wanted her to have a piece of Mom."

Now it was Granny's turn to tear up. She sniffled and sent Claire a smile. "Oh, Mona would have loved that. It's not quite as good as Margaret, but I'll take it." Then, she gazed at the baby once more. "What do you think of your name—Rosemarie Mona Kane, Princess of Amorley?"

The baby yawned in response, her eyes still closed.

Granny's eyes flitted toward Claire. "She is a princess, right—or did I get the title wrong? I can't keep track of who is a duchess or duke or whatever else. It doesn't matter much to me because she'll always be my little Rosemarie."

Ethan chuckled. "Yes, she's a princess." He leaned closer to Claire and gave her hand another kiss. "You did a smashing job. Are you feeling all right?"

Claire pushed herself up higher in the bed and winced. "I'm fine. I mean, not fine—everything hurts, but I'm thankful that Rosemarie and I made it through this unscathed, and it's over. What about the weather? Has the storm stopped?"

"Let me check with Nigel. Perhaps he got through to someone. He said he would look at the landline phone and see if he could get the power working." Ethan released her hand after planting his lips on it once more and then left the room.

Claire rested her head on her pillow and closed her eyes. She silently thanked God for making it through the labor and delivery and had almost drifted to sleep when someone shook her shoulder fiercely.

"Claire, wake up. Open your eyes. I need your help," Granny's voice filled with panic.

Sitting upright in the bed, Claire's eyes shot open, and her heart pounded like she'd run a marathon. "What's wrong?" Her eyes adjusted to the light, and she searched her granny's face for answers.

Granny shoved Rosemarie's head onto Claire's lap. "Look. Her lips—they look blue. They aren't supposed to look like that, are they?"

Claire's heart clenched, and for a few seconds, she couldn't breathe. "No." The baby's nostrils flared and confirmed her granny's concerns—Rosemarie's lips had a slightly bluish tint, and she struggled to breathe. Claire whispered, "Go get Ethan. See if you can find a bulb syringe, a first aid kit, or emergency medical equipment."

Ethan rushed into the room, and his eyes widened

with worry. "What should we do?"

Claire continued to count the infant's respiratory rate in her head, keeping her eyes on the second hand of a clock in the room. "Too fast. She's breathing too fast. We must get her down this mountain and to a hospital ASAP."

Claire ran through her emergency medical training for resuscitating a newborn and considered all the possible differentials. It could be transient tachypnea, but she also recalled that delivering at higher altitudes could cause shunting and cause the blue appearance to Rosemarie's lips. Either way, if she could get oxygen on the baby, things would most likely improve. They didn't have a lot of time to waste.

Ethan ran a hand through his hair. "There has to be something in the way of a vehicle that we can use around here. I'll go out and search around the cabin one more time. Maybe I overlooked something last night."

Wilson darted into the room. He came to Claire's bedside and rested his head on her thigh. Sniffing at the infant, he looked up at Claire and barked before nudging her hand toward the baby.

"He's worried, too." She scratched his head with her free hand and leaned closer to him. "Go help your dad find us a way out of here."

He sat up straight and barked again as if accepting his mission, then he trotted out the door, not waiting for her husband. Ethan's brow furrowed. "I'll be right back." He ran out of the room, leaving Claire alone to fret over her baby's future.

~

Ethan trudged through the snow, his eyes scanning the landscape for any indication of human life or some semblance of activity aside from the gentle snowfall and occasional squirrel playing on tree limbs overhead.

Wilson trotted beside him, looking happy to be outdoors.

Sweat beaded Ethan's forehead and the back of his neck, and he wiped it away to keep it from obscuring his vision. Glancing down at his canine companion, he reminded the dog and himself, "We have to get help fast. Claire and the baby are counting on us."

The dog barked in agreement as if he'd understood the mission he'd been given and broke into a run.

"Wilson, wait!" Ethan didn't have time to chase down the rambunctious dog today. He had to find a way down the mountain but couldn't return to Claire and tell her that he'd lost her furry friend. Shouting for the dog a few more times, Ethan had almost given up on his effort when Wilson bounded out of some brush in the forest.

The dog shook snow that clung to his nose, ears, and coat. He repeatedly barked, refusing to stop. When Ethan didn't move, Wilson joined him at his side and latched on to his pant leg, tugging on it.

The force caused Ethan to topple over, and he put his hand down to break his fall. "Ouch. What are you doing? We have to find help. No one's around. I'm going to hike down the mountain, I guess." He stared at the dog, praying for a way out of their mess.

Again, Wilson grabbed onto Ethan's pants and yanked hard. Then he released them and barked again.

"What is it, Wilson? Did you find something? Did something scare you in the forest?" Ethan glanced around, searching for the source of Wilson's aggravation. He rose from the ground and brushed the snow off before returning his attention to the dog again.

The dog barked again and grabbed Ethan's leg a third time.

Ethan raised his hands in defeat. "All right. I'll come to see what it is, but we have to hurry." With this concession, Wilson bounded away. Ethan had to break into a slight jog that turned into a full-out run to keep pace with the animal.

When the pair arrived at a clearing in the forest, Ethan stopped, winded, and panic took over. Time was slipping away, and he had to save his daughter. He rested his hands on his thighs and hunched forward, sucking in air. "I don't see anything. What has you so upset?" he stuttered between gasps.

Wilson jogged over to something covered in pine branches, tree limbs, and a good mound of snow. The dog lay on the ground, jutting his nose toward the mass.

Ethan walked over to the pile of debris and snow and peered down at the dog again. "You want me to do something with this? It's just a bunch of wood."

Wilson barked again, but he didn't stop this time.

Ethan shook his head but indulged the dog. He dusted the snow off the mound and then lifted branches and twigs off the object they concealed. A weathered red snowmobile sat underneath the debris.

Ethan's hands dropped to his side, and he turned to look at his canine friend. "You found this? How did you find this?"

In response, Wilson moved to a sitting position, grinned, and wagged his tail.

Ethan leaned closer to the machine, inspecting it for functionality. It didn't look to be in too bad of shape. His eyes landed on a set of keys in the ignition, and his heart stopped. This could be their way down the mountain and to the help that his baby required.

He reached down and turned the key. "Please, God, let it start." After a few failed attempts, the engine roared to life. Ethan punched his fist in the air. "Yes!" He turned and looked at Wilson. "Come on. Get in. We don't have much time."

Wilson obliged and jumped aboard the rusty chariot, giving Ethan a bark of approval. Ethan scratched the dog's head. "You did great. Way to save the day."

Wilson smiled and gave Ethan a lick on the cheek.

Pressing down on the gas, the snowmobile lurched forward, and the duo hurried back to the cabin as fast as the machine would carry them. Snow blew past his face, and Ethan squinted, struggling to make out the path he'd taken from the cabin through the woods.

Countless minutes later, they arrived at the cabin's front door where Ethan had left his wife and struggling newborn. He held his breath, opened the front door, and rushed in, praying that the baby was still alive. "Claire," he called, "I'm back. I found a way out of here."

Granny hurried to him and grabbed him by the arm. "They're ready. I believed the Lord would provide a way, so I told Claire to bundle up the baby. Good thing I did, too, because God came through like He always does."

Ethan dashed to the bedroom where he'd left his little family. He entered the room, and his eyes landed on Claire, who held the new baby in her arms, staring carefully at the infant's face.

She lifted her head and met his gaze. "Oh, thank goodness, you made it back."

He waved for her to follow him. "Hurry. I found a snowmobile. Let's get her to help."

Claire didn't pause to ask any questions. Instead, she jumped into action and followed her husband out of the cabin.

They jumped onto the beacon of hope that resembled more of a rusted tractor, Claire uttering prayers of gratitude for the rescue.

Granny called behind them, "Get that baby help fast and send someone for the rest of us as soon as possible. I don't like being away from you for too long. You might need Ole Granny."

~

Tears stung Claire's eyes. She blew a kiss with one hand and watched over her shoulder as her granny and Nigel standing at the front door grew smaller. Did Nigel place an arm around Granny? No, she must be hallucinating. Nigel was probably picking something off her granny's shoulder.

Ethan zipped down the mountain, veering around bumps along the way. Snow flew in their eyes, and the cold air stung their noses.

Claire held the baby closer and monitored for any acute changes. So far, Rosemarie had fighter qualities. "Come on, baby. You can do it. You're strong. You're a Thomson woman." Claire had found a pulse oximeter in an emergency kit at the cabin buried in the bottom of a closet. Still nasal flaring, the baby didn't respond to her request, but her oxygen saturation stayed around 90-92 %, and she remained stable.

An agonizing twenty minutes later, they pulled in front of the Grand Royal International Hotel. Lunging off the snowmobile, Ethan ran to the other side and helped Claire out, scooping the baby in his arms.

Wilson bounded out of the machine and jogged behind the trio. He ran into the lodge, and Claire hurried alongside him. The minute she entered the lodge, Claire yelled, disregarding royal formality or social etiquette, "My baby needs help. Call 911. Tell them we need an ambulance. Newborn with hypoxia."

Several staffers in black suits sprang up behind the glossy mahogany desk. One hour later, the ambulance whisked Claire, Ethan, and Rosemarie into the local hospital's emergency department.

"I can't believe we got here so quickly." Claire hovered over her baby, smoothing her hand across the infant's cheek, which now had oxygen tubing taped in place. "At least she's improved. Her oxygen saturation level is normal with the supplemental oxygen, and her color looks good. Nice and pink." Unimpressed with the attention, Rosemarie yawned.

Ethan stepped closer to his wife and placed a hand on his daughter's head. "She is beautiful." He glanced at Claire. "Just like her mother."

Claire's face flushed, and she smiled. "Aw, thanks. I'm glad we reached the hospital in time. She scared me to death. Thank you for being our hero." She stretched up on her tiptoes and planted a kiss on her husband's lips.

Someone rapped on the door, and the couple stepped apart. Claire cleared her throat. "Come in."

The door opened, and the doctor who'd tended to Rosemarie entered the room. He adjusted his glasses and glanced at the infant's vitals. "How's my famous patient doing?"

Ethan glanced at his wife and daughter. "She's much better, thank you."

Still resting her hand on her daughter's cheek, Claire asked the doctor, "How did her lab work and chest x-ray look?"

The doctor glanced at the patient's chart.

"Everything looks good. There are no signs of infection, and the oxygen seems to be helping. Her x-ray appears clear, but I'm waiting for the radiologist's final read. I'd like to keep her overnight, maybe even for forty-eight hours, for observation and wait until the blood cultures come back."

Claire shifted her weight and glanced at her husband. "That sounds fine. I'd rather be certain she's okay."

Ethan nodded. "Whatever you think is best, we will do."

The doctor studied Rosemarie's monitors once more. "Let's keep her for the forty-eight hours then, and if everything else comes back normal, she can go home—just in time for the Fruhling Gala." He sent Claire a smile.

"Right. Well, thank you again." Claire dipped her head in a nod to the kind doctor.

He gave a small bow and left the room, shutting the door behind him.

As soon as he'd gone, Claire turned to her husband. "I completely forgot about the Fruhling Gala. It slipped my mind between labor, delivery, and that harrowing trek down the mountain. How is that possible?"

Ethan chuckled. "A lot has happened. It's understandable."

Her brow furrowing, Claire chewed on her thumbnail. "How will we be ready to cohost the

Fruhling Gala? Plus, there's no guarantee Rosemarie will be released from the hospital by then, and I don't want to leave her to go to some party. There's no way."

Ethan's gaze settled upon his worried wife. "There's something else."

Claire frowned. "What else could possibly have gone wrong?"

"Um, well, when we first arrived at the hospital, one of the nurses said something to me that I found odd. I didn't think much of it then because I was so worried about Rosemarie. However, when I momentarily stepped out of the room to find the doctor, another nurse said it surprised her to see that you were alive. The news has reported that you…died."

Claire's jaw dropped. "What? I died? I didn't die. How ridiculous."

"I thought so, too, but I asked her where she got her information, and she said the news had been reporting for the last day that you'd died in the snow squall. Gone missing or something."

Claire felt her face heat up. "Why would they say that? We weren't missing that long. Who could have spread a rumor like that?"

Squeezing his wife's shoulders, he leaned closer. "Don't worry about it right now. Let's get through the next two days, and then we will deal with the gala. It will all work out—you'll see."

She laid her head on her husband's chest and sighed. "I hope you're right."

~

Over the next few hours, Claire's phone dinged every few seconds from social media. She'd ignored most of the dings because of her concern over Rosemarie.

After the five-hundredth one, she pulled the phone out of her purse and tapped the social media site with the highest notification count. Her eyes landed on an unflattering picture of herself chasing Wilson across the field at the dog show. The caption read, *Did Our Queen Run Away?* Below the photo, an article discussed the likelihood of her demise on the mountain versus whether she staged her disappearance and left the country. It questioned her leadership ability if she indeed had survived the snowsquall, and if not, it suggested alternative leadership.

Tacky. What if she'd died on the mountain?

Her eyes flitted up toward Ethan's face. "Nice. I'm either a deadbeat leader, or they didn't let my body cool before discussing my replacement. I still don't know exactly what Maurelle's play would have been other than some sort of deal with Maltenstein for power."

Ethan nodded. "The last time she tried to take over with Lord Chicanery from Maltenstein, she sent them money. Maybe she's up to her old tricks again."

Claire tilted her head and considered this point. Her hands were still frozen like permanent popsicles. When she shoved them inside her coat to warm them, her fingers bumped into a crumpled piece of paper. She pulled it out. "What's this?"

Ethan shrugged. "Looks like trash."

Unfolding it, Claire's eyes skimmed the document. A few seconds later, she gasped. Shoving it in front of Ethan, her hand shook. "It's a letter to Maurelle. Read it."

*Dear Maurelle,*

*As you know, previous efforts to intertwine our countries have failed. This effort must succeed. I remind you that we will ensure your future rise to power and our continued protection in exchange for your continued financial support. It will advantage us both to see Claire removed from power. For both our countries and families, we cannot fail. Use any means necessary.*

*Sincerely,*
*King Spickletz*

"Talk about a smoking gun. But how did it get in your coat?" Ethan frowned.

Claire pinched her brow, thinking. Of course. "From Fraulein Halstaff. She must have been the intermediary between Maurelle and King Spickletz. I bet she wore the coat herself, shoved it in the pocket, and forgot about it."

Ethan opened his mouth to say something further, but his phone rang. He opened the social media site and clicked on Notifications. "Oh, look. You're alive now, according to major media outlets." He turned his phone screen around to face her.

She sent him a wry smile. "Super." Claire rubbed her chapped lips with her knuckle, considering her next move. "I'm tired of this—of getting pushed around. It's time to take charge of the situation. Boldness, right? Courage?"

Ethan smiled cautiously. "Yes, but what are you going to do?"

Claire opened her contact list on her phone and made a phone call. "Hello. This is the queen of Amorley. Please gather the press and prepare for a briefing outside the hospital." She paused and listened to the Intercontinental Games President's response. "Thank you. I will see you in thirty minutes."

Turning the phone off, Claire glanced at her husband again. "There. It's done. I'm addressing the world about this nonsense in thirty minutes. Can't help but think someone planned all of this—maybe not the snowstorm—but somehow, this rumor about us got started, and I have an idea who the culprit is."

Ethan frowned. "You don't think she—"

"I do." Claire crossed her arms. "Maurelle." She gathered her purse, squared her shoulders, and marched out of the hospital, ready to reclaim her throne.

# Chapter 16

Claire stood in front of the hospital, ready to address the press she'd called to her impromptu public address. She cleared her throat and straightened her posture.

Before she could step forward to the microphone stand placed a few feet away, the Intercontinental Games president rushed toward her. His face had drained of color. He leaned his head close to hers and hissed, "We were told you were dead!"

The king of Maltenstein hurried to Claire's side as well. He whispered, "That's right. How were we to know that you'd survived the squall? The weather took a horrible turn, and we received some information that you, Ethan, and your granny hadn't made it out in time."

Neither gentleman realized the microphone had been turned on already. Their voices echoed throughout the crowd, giving them pause.

The audience murmured, and several members of the press nodded.

Claire's stomach plummeted. "As Mark Twain once said, 'Reports of my death have been exaggerated.' These reports don't make sense to me. We were missing only a few days."

The president of the games rubbed his bearded chin. "Yes, well, as soon as the storm hit, most of the crowd attending the downhill ski event made it to safety. We became concerned when you and your party didn't return."

Claire raised a hand, hardly able to hear anymore. She stepped forward, grasping hold of the microphone and clearing her throat. "It's come to my attention that my character and leadership ability have been questioned. I've been told that people have said in my absence that I no longer care about my country and am incompetent, inconsiderate, and incapable of leading appropriately and effectively." She stopped speaking and let her eyes scan the crowd, allowing them to linger a few seconds longer on the Maltenstein leaders' faces.

Shock jolted her. Was that Maurelle? She blinked hard to clear her eyes, looking again. But the person had vanished, so she continued, "That is not the case, let me assure you. Unfortunately, I could not attend the beginning of the Intercontinental Games as I had to focus on my health and the wellness of my unborn baby—the future heir to the Amorley throne. As a result, I also missed the closing ceremony of the Intercontinental Games because my family and I remained stranded on the mountain when the snow squall hit, and then I had my baby.

"These unforeseeable events hindered my ability to participate as I would have liked, and it grieved my spirit to miss cheering on my fellow citizens in the games."

The small crowd nodded, and a few murmurs spread through the audience.

Claire squeezed her hands together, gathering the courage to press onward. "Also, I would never do anything to harm someone else. Certainly not the citizens of Amorley, but I believe the Maltenstein leaders and Maurelle Evercliff would like you to believe that I've lost interest in the advancement of Amorley."

She swallowed hard, her hands shaking in anger. "This is also not true. Sometimes, things may not be as they appear, and I would ask you to extend to me the trust earned over the past year. Some of my actions may be rooted in reasons beyond what is visible on the surface but are vital to our country's well-being."

Glancing over her shoulder at the Intercontinental Games president and the king of Maltenstein, Claire frowned and placed her hand on her hip. "Who told you I had died? How would anyone know about my family's whereabouts? At the very least, you could have sent out a search party and not given up hope on the queen of Amorley and her potential heir so quickly." *Yeah, right.* If she and her family were out of the way, it would have set up the Maltenstein faction to acquire her country's power and resources easily.

"Well, I'd rather not say where the information came from, but—"

The president of the Intercontinental Games interjected, "Here's a possibility. I overheard a conversation between the king of Maltenstein and a dark-haired woman in the main lodge. I remember her because she had long red fingernails and an unusual slithering gait."

*Maurelle*. It had to be her. Claire's palms dampened. "Do you recall her name?"

The man squinted his eyes, taking a moment to respond, "Maurelle. I almost couldn't believe it to be true. I didn't say something sooner because I hadn't seen her face."

"What did she say exactly?" Claire's jaw tightened, half-afraid to hear the answer.

"She said that a transition of power would be simple with the little one and her insipid daughter-in-law out of the way. There was something about how she didn't think King Spickletz could pull it off but that he'd been right to send Fraulein Halstaff as a spy. Then she said things couldn't have worked out more smoothly if they'd planned for the storm."

The crowd wore horrified expressions, and a low rumble of voices launched.

Claire raised her hand, silencing them again. "I don't understand something—there's no way Maurelle or the Maltenstein rulers could have known that the squall was coming. They couldn't control the weather."

From the rear of the crowd, a ruckus commenced, and Claire's eyes shifted to the disturbance.

A voice cut through the chaos and pierced Claire's soul. "Let go of me."

A few gentlemen had a woman in hand, flanking either side of her.

The crowd parted, and Claire's eyes landed on the source of the interruption.

*Maurelle.*

Claire's stepmother struggled against the two men holding her arms. "I said let go of me. Do you know who I am?" She turned her attention to Claire and glared at her.

Claire's heart pounded hard in her chest. "Wha– what are you doing here?"

Maurelle stood stoic and silent.

Her throat tightened, but Claire pressed on, "I asked what you are doing here. Is it true? Did you construct all of this to take over the throne?"

Maurelle narrowed her eyes further. "I admit nothing. It would not be my fault if the king of Maltenstein or the Intercontinental Games president neglected the most recent weather forecast on the day in question. Perhaps, the final event should have been moved to another day. Perhaps the forecaster knew a storm was coming. Of course, it would be a shame if the people in charge of your transportation misunderstood their assignment for the day in case of emergency. Also, it would be equally terrible if your group became isolated and unable to escape the storm with the rest of the attendees. Again, this is all speculation. However, in the event of your untimely death, then I, as the wife of the former king of Amorley, should be the queen, and my son should be the heir apparent."

Claire's shook her head. "None of this makes sense. We've been through this many times. You can't rule. You don't have a blood-lineage claim to the throne. Eric could, but I don't know if he'd even agree. What was your plan for that problem?"

From amidst the crowd, Michael caught Claire's eye. "I know the answer to that question. Using my parliament connections, I discovered that Maurelle paid off many Parliament members to ensure that if she made a final play for the crown, there would be a referendum to change the constitution."

Claire's jaw dropped, and she shielded her eyes to see Maurelle. "No," she whispered. "You would have let me and my unborn child perish on that mountain? For what? Power? Money? Is it all worth it?"

Maurelle's face twisted into a serpentine grin. "Again, I admit nothing but ousting your pretty little face from the throne you stole from my son and me? Absolutely. Anything would be worth that."

The look on Maurelle's face and her sharp words caused the blood in Claire's veins to turn cold. She shivered. It was hard to imagine someone having so much hate in their heart towards another person that they'd go to such lengths to destroy that person, but here Claire stood—right smack in the middle of her fairy tale-turned-nightmare.

Claire closed her eyes and whispered, "God, give me the grace to withstand this. Help me to find forgiveness for her and not let bitterness fill my soul." Then, she opened her eyes and let her gaze settle on her stepmother. "I forgive you."

Maurelle stared hard at Claire. "What kind of ridiculous statement is that?"

"It's not ridiculous." Claire sucked in a deep breath and exhaled slowly before continuing, "It's the truth. I don't want to hate you, wish bad things for you, or let anything vile fill my heart. You will still have to answer to the law for treason, but I can honestly say that I forgive you because God has forgiven me. So, there. I forgive you."

Maurelle snorted and flailed against the two gentlemen flanking her sides, who secured her arms.

The crowd yelled, "Treason," chanting the words over and over.

She spit out her following words, "I should have been the queen. Not you. Go back to your little hospital." She shot a final, scathing look toward Claire.

The men tightened their grip and turned Maurelle around. They led her through the crowd and out of Claire's vicinity.

Claire's shoulders sagged as soon as her

stepmother faded from her view. She quickly realized that everyone had shifted their attention back to her.

*Oh no.* Tomorrow was the Fruhling Gala. She'd forgotten about it between almost turning into a popsicle on a mountain and ensuring her newborn survived her first week of life.

She could not let herself fall apart yet. Her duty to Amorley and her family came first. Claire cleared her throat. "Please excuse the interruption. I appreciate your patience and support. We will not let this disheartening news ruin the end of the spectacular Intercontinental Games. Tomorrow night is a big event, and I want everyone to enjoy it. Go home and remember what's important—God, love, and family. I will see you all at the Fruhling Gala and introduce you to Rosemarie Mona Kane."

The photographers' flashes popped throughout the crowd, and the public broke into a low roar with a mishmash of questions and exclamations. Claire waved as her grandmother had taught her and exited the stage.

As soon as she escaped the public's view, she collapsed into Ethan's arms and sobbed.

Her tears held a mixture of relief that the announcement was over, disappointment that her stepmother held so much rancor, and unease that Maurelle's conspirators still abounded. She sputtered between cries, "I still don't know how we're going to be ready for the Gala tomorrow."

Ethan held her close, stroking her hair, and

whispered in her ear, "It's going to be all right. You're safe."

After several minutes her sobs subsided. A few scattered hiccups replaced her cries, and she eventually pulled away from Ethan and wiped the tears off her cheeks with her fingertips. Sucking in a deep breath, she released it and rolled her shoulders back.

He raised a brow, his hands still resting on her shoulders, steadying her. Handing her a tissue that he'd dug out of his pocket, he asked, "Better?"

She chuckled and swiped her nose with the tissue. "I think so. Thanks."

"You're welcome." He grinned. "I have good news."

Claire smiled. "That's great. I could use some good news. What is it?"

Before Ethan could answer, a familiar voice interrupted their conversation, "Darling, you cannot be serious? I'm gone for a short time, and this is how you dress? Have I taught you nothing?"

Claire whipped around.

Standing before her was a fashionable woman dressed in white from head to toe. She wore a swooping, oversized hat cocked to one side and heels that added five inches to her small stature.

"Mademoiselle Couture. It's good to see you." Claire couldn't help herself. She'd never been so glad to see the fashionista, and she rushed over and flung her arms around the French woman's neck.

"Oof. I can't breathe. You're squeezing the air out of me. Honestly, I've always taught you to maintain decorum. This display of emotion is wholly unnecessary, and I—"

Claire released her former stylist and instructor on all things designer and beamed.

The woman stared at Claire's tear-stained face and broke into a wide grin. "—I'm glad to see you, too. Thankfully, I brought many options for tomorrow's gala, and it looks like I arrived just in time. What hack dressed you in my absence?"

Claire sent her a half-grin. "Fraulein Halstaff from Maltenstein."

Mademoiselle Couture rolled her eyes. "Oh, please. That woman. She wouldn't know good taste if it landed in her lap. She's copied other stylists for years, including me. Fortunately, now you have the original rather than the duplicate." She gestured toward herself as if on display and paused for a moment before clapping her hands together. "Laisse-le-moi. We must hurry. Let's head to the hotel and begin. We have a lot of work to do." She spun around and marched away, assuming everyone would fall in line. After a few steps, however, she paused and glanced over her shoulder. "Oh, and I must see that baby before we get to work."

Claire grinned. "Of course." Then, she jumped into line behind Mademoiselle Couture and returned to the hotel, ready to demonstrate her rightful place as the head of her country.

# Chapter 17

Ethan stuck his head through the crack in the door to the master bedroom. "How are things coming?" He'd picked up many American sayings from Claire, and this one he found particularly useful. It was an excellent way of hurrying others along. He glanced at his watch.

Granny waved a hand at him. "We know. We know. The Fruhling Gala begins in one hour. We still have time."

"*Pas assez*. I need a month to prepare for this event, but alas, *c'est la vie*—we must make do with the time we've been given." Mademoiselle Couture frowned, her eyes scanning over Claire's dress. "What is it you Americans say? It could be worse."

Claire snorted. "Thanks—and yes, that is the correct, if not insulting, use of that statement."

Ethan chuckled, stepping further into the room. "Ignore her. You look fantastic. Of course, you'd look gorgeous in anything."

Claire studied her reflection in the mirror that

Mademoiselle Couture's staff had placed before her, taking in the overall look. Ethan hadn't lied. She didn't know how Mademoiselle Couture had worked a miracle in such a short amount of time, but she and her black-suited, heeled minions had done it.

Claire wore a sapphire velvet gown that graced her body, skimming the floor. It had a train that provided a dramatic effect but also concerned Claire because she didn't have the best track record with walking, much less in heels while dodging a runner of fabric behind her. She turned to face Mademoiselle Couture. Patting her chignon that one of the stylists had concocted, Claire smiled. "It's perfect. Thank you. I'll do my best to wear it well and walk with sure steps tonight."

In her stoic and usual apathetic expression, Mademoiselle Couture pursed her lips and gave a slight nod. "See that you do. That gown cost more than you can imagine, and I must return it intact by tomorrow morning to the designer who loaned it to us. That means no canine mishaps, no spills, and no tears. Understand?" She arched a brow, waiting for Claire's response.

"Absolutely. I'll take good care of it. Promise." She crossed her heart with her finger.

As if on cue, Wilson bounded into the room, followed closely by Nigel, who wore a ruddy, sweaty face and an expression of aggravation. "Get back here right now. We don't have time for this. Heel. Sit. Stay. Oh, just don't move."

Wilson glanced at Nigel as if considering whether to acquiesce. Still, after a few seconds of debate, he chose the more fun option and continued terrorizing Mademoiselle Couture and her staff.

Mademoiselle Couture shrieked as the dog jumped in and out of her staffers' legs and then dove for the black clutch Claire had planned to carry that night. He held it between his teeth, lowered his head in a playful pose, and wagged his tail back and forth. Her canine had issued a challenge.

Claire raised a hand. "Don't move. He'll—"

Before she could salvage the situation, Nigel yelled at the dog. "You listen to me. Get back here right now. I—" He lunged forward, aiming for the clutch and the dog.

Challenge accepted. Wilson shot off for the open door and jetted down the hallway and out of sight.

Claire sighed. So much for the clutch. She glanced at Mademoiselle Couture.

Fumes could have billowed out of the fashion guru's ears. Her face had shifted to a shade beyond red, landing in the zone of eggplant.

*Yikes.* Claire stepped off the pedestal set up in her bedroom, careful not to snag her heel on the bottom of the dress. "Uh. Sorry. But at least he didn't damage the dress. Right? That's progress. Besides, we can find another purse for me to carry or scrap the purse altogether. I don't need it. I have a diaper bag and—"

"A diaper bag. What is this diaper bag?"

Mademoiselle Couture stepped forward.

*Uh-oh.* The French might frown on the handy-dandy, multiuse carryall she'd found and filled with all her favorite things in preparation for the baby. Pragmatic was Claire's middle name. Sure, the bag wouldn't be seen on the spring-fashion runways, but she had to have things for the baby—diapers, wipes, pacifiers. "Well, uh, it's a bag to hold all the baby's things. You know—a diaper bag." She turned around and moved over to her closet, where she'd stashed the bag so it would be ready when the baby arrived. Pulling it out of the bottom of the closet, she held it up in the air. "Here. See?"

Mademoiselle Couture's hand flew to their chest at the sight of the brown quilted bag with its thick nylon strap. "*Oh la la la la.* No. That will not do."

Claire glanced at her bag and shrugged. It looked okay to her.

Mademoiselle Couture sighed and extended a hand. "Give it to me. Must I fix everything?" she huffed, murmuring a stream of French phrases.

Obliging, Claire relinquished the offensive bag and stood by while the army of stylists rearranged her things into a more fashionable, acceptable carryall that resembled a high-end designer bag more than a diaper sack.

Giving the new bag to Claire, Mademoiselle Couture pursed her lips. "*Voilà.* Do not ever let me see that—" Her eyes flicked to the discarded diaper bag in the corner of the room, "—thing ever again." She met Claire's gaze and gave her one final scan. "Good. You look *magnifique*. I am a miracle worker, *n'est-ce pas*?"

Claire smiled. Mademoiselle Couture didn't lack confidence. Some people probably found it off-putting, but it had always amused Claire. "You are. Thank you—for everything." Overcome with emotion from all she'd endured the past few days, Claire stepped forward and threw her arms around the fashion guru.

"Oof," Mademoiselle Couture heaved. She patted the Amorley ruler on the back. "There, there. That's enough of that. You're welcome. I consider it my duty to ensure that you represent Amorley well. Even though it is not my home country, I've grown fond of it."

Claire sighed and released Mademoiselle Couture.

The petite woman sent her a wink. "Now, you must go. You will be beyond late. There's fashionably late, then there's rude, and we cannot have that." She clapped her hands, and the fashion regiment jumped into action, gathering their supplies and extra outfits.

Within minutes the entire room had cleared, leaving Claire to stand alone in front of the mirror in her room.

Gazing at her reflection, she patted her hair and twisted side to side for one final inspection. Mademoiselle Couture was right—she did look good. Only one thing left to do—represent Amorley to the best of her ability at the Fruhling Gala and solidify her place in history as her country's ruler. She wouldn't let

Maurelle, the Maltenstein crew, or anyone else hurt her family or government again. Not ever.

# Chapter 18

Pacing the floor to the side of the stage, Ethan stared at his watch one more time. Twenty minutes late. Claire had told him to go on to the Fruhling Gala and stall for time while she finished getting ready at the hotel. He'd hesitantly obliged. After all they had been through, he didn't want to leave her alone, lest an avalanche hit the building, or an unannounced family member arrive and plot to steal the throne. However, she'd insisted. Still, given the extent of her tardiness, he'd begun to worry. Again, he glanced down at his wrist.

A breathless voice interrupted his worry, "I'm here. Sorry that I'm so late."

He raised his gaze, and his eyes landed on his wife, who looked more beautiful than he'd ever seen her. Perhaps it was the glow of motherhood or the fact that he'd almost lost her, but he'd never seen Claire shine like tonight. Her cheeks flushed a rosy pink, and her blue eyes shone brightly. "You look gorgeous. Spectacular." He leaned forward and planted a soft kiss on her cheek.

Claire sent him a smile and pushed a loose tendril out of her face. "Thanks. You do, too. Handsome, I mean." Her cheeks flushed.

Ethan grinned, pleased that he could still fluster her a bit. "Thank you." He turned and peered at the empty stage. "You'd better get up there. The crowd has been growing restless."

She nodded and swallowed hard.

Ethan reached over and took her hand in his, giving it a squeeze. No matter how often she did it, his wife hated public speaking. He caught her gaze. "You're going to do great. Just speak from your heart. Don't be afraid."

"Right." She released his hand and closed her eyes briefly before opening them and taking the stairs to the awaiting stage.

~

Claire's hands shook, and her palms sweated. Last night, she'd tossed and turned, unable to sleep. After hours spent in prayer, asking God for guidance as to how to proceed today, one thought became clear—she'd had enough of the subterfuge. It was time to take her place as the rightful queen of Amorley once and for all. Even though she'd made the press aware of her survival of the snowstorm, she still had much to say on the matter.

After reflecting on her conversation with Maurelle and turning over the events that had transpired between

Maurelle and the king of Maltenstein, Claire came to a conclusion. The public deserved to hear the truth, and as their leader, she wouldn't stand by and have her leadership threatened any longer.

Her husband's reassuring touch still lingered in her mind, but it didn't subside her nerves as she prepared to address the crowd filled with her fellow citizens and a large faction from Maltenstein.

Stepping toward the awaiting podium, she took one last deep breath and released it. *Please help me be brave, God.* She placed her hands on either side of the podium and let her eyes skim the crowd. The ballroom hosting the Fruhling Gala looked magnificent. The glitter of multiple chandeliers cast a soft golden glow across the room. The black and white marble floor added the clink-clink of footsteps from the well-heeled women crossing its surface to carry on conversations and dance. The aroma of cinnamon-infused baked goods filled the air, intermixed with a savory scent of roasted turkey and mulled cider. Red roses on tables at the room's periphery added a romantic dash of color and promised romance and drama. The venue couldn't have been more perfect for the fancy springtime event.

Claire gripped the podium a bit tighter and cleared her throat. "Good evening."

The crowd fell silent, and the clinking of glasses and the dull roar of chatter halted.

"Welcome to the Fruhling Gala, an event created to celebrate unity between countries, particularly

Maltenstein and Amorley." She smiled and waited for the crowd to receive her greeting.

Several audience members from Amorley smiled and nodded while most of the Maltenstein group frowned or stood with stoic expressions.

"As much as I had hoped that this evening would bring peace and unity, I regret to inform you that will not be the case." Claire let her gaze shift and settle on the face of King Spickletz and his wife.

The crowd collectively gasped.

"This may shock some of you, but my family and I remained trapped on the mountaintop during the recent snow squall."

Murmurs circulated the room, and many of the audience nodded, indicating they'd been aware of her plight.

"Fortunately, we made it out of the experience alive, despite me having to deliver my daughter there. As many of you know, my daughter suffered a tenuous entry into the world. By the way, she is doing well now and has fully recovered." Claire smiled and waited while the audience digested this information.

"Unfortunately, the Maltenstein rulers thwarted any rescue attempts."

More gasps ensued.

Claire clasped her hands and gathered her courage. "We've since learned they were working with my stepmother, Maurelle Evercliff, to help her take over as leader of Amorley by pushing my future heir and me aside by any means necessary. I have learned Maltenstein's leadership intended to replace me with Maurelle under the guise of having her son take the throne once my family and I were out of the way. In the past, she has signed agreements and made exchanges with Maltenstein leadership, indicating that if she or her son ever rose to power, then she would exchange Amorley's financial resources for Maltenstein's power and support."

Standing in the front row, the queen mother's face went pale. She clutched her purse closer to her body and hurried up the stairs to the stage where Claire stood. Once she got close enough to speak to Claire, she asked, "What? You mean she intended to get rid of you—for good?"

Her voice echoed over the crowd and startled Claire and the queen mother.

Claire's gaze landed on her royal grandmother. "Yes. She wanted my daughter and me out of the way—permanently."

The queen mother's hand flew to her chest. "Oh, dear. I can hardly believe it." She remained by her granddaughter's side, placing a hand on her shoulder in an uncharacteristic but welcome display of affection and support.

Turning her attention to her audience, Claire continued, "I found a document she had signed agreeing to a union between herself and the Maltenstein rulers. She promised them access to Amorley's coffers as long as they assisted with her efforts to remove me and secure her son, thereby assuring her access to power in Amorley."

A wave of uproar coursed through the crowd.

After a few seconds, Claire tapped on the microphone to regain the crowd's attention. "I know this is hard to digest, but when I took my vow as your queen, I pledged to honor and protect Amorley and the interests of its inhabitants." She sent a pointed stare at the Maltenstein king and queen. "That is exactly what I intend to do. Therefore, as of today, there will be no financial or other support from Amorley to Maltenstein. As of this day, consider you and your country warned. We will not back down. We will not be intimidated. We will stand for truth, honor, and courage.

"As for tonight, I encourage everyone to enjoy the evening and would ask the Maltenstein rulers to please see themselves out posthaste, as my country has fully funded this function. And you are not welcome." With her final words, Claire stepped away from the podium, her hands still shaking. She crossed the stage, took each stair carefully, and made it to the floor in one piece. She'd done it. *Thank you, God.*

Ethan awaited below and wrapped her in an embrace. Whispering in her ear, he leaned close. "You did a wonderful job."

She closed her eyes and relaxed her shoulders, grateful to have her family intact, and her country secured. "Thank you. I couldn't do any of this without you."

He leaned back and stared into her eyes. "Yes, you could, but you don't have to, and I'm happy to be along for the adventure."

Cooing behind Claire caught her attention. She turned to see the source of the sweet noises. "There's my beautiful girl."

Rosemarie lay in Granny's arms, wrapped in a soft white blanket and wearing a cap with a mini-fascinator on her head.

Claire smirked. "Nice hat."

Granny cackled. "Old Mademoiselle Couture thought so, too. That lady drives me crazy most of the time, but I've got to hand it to her. This baby's outfit is pretty snazzy. It doesn't hurt that she matches me, either."

Claire's eyes drifted to her granny's attire. She wore a white suit jacket, skirt, black heels, and a white fascinator hat that eerily emulated the one on Claire's daughter's head. Full-out belly laughs ensued. "Oh my, those hats are the best things I have ever seen."

Nigel joined them and stood close to her granny. "I have to agree." His eyes locked with Claire's granny and lingered on her longer than necessary.

An idea tickled Claire's brain. "Wait a minute. Am I missing something?" She pointed her finger between the pair. "Is something going on here between the two of you?"

In all of her life, Claire had never seen Granny

redden, but today, her face flushed a deep crimson color, and she sputtered, "Well, uh…you see, we both had been meaning to discuss with you. It's just with everything going on, and the snow thing, and then the gala, and uh—"

Nigel stepped forward. "Margaret is trying to say that I have fallen in love with this beautiful woman, and today I asked her to marry me."

Claire's jaw dropped. "What?" She turned to face her granny. "For real?"

Her granny rocked the baby side to side and frowned. "Well, uh, yes. For real. As long as you are all right with it. I don't want you to be upset. You and I have been a little family for years—the Thomson girls against the world, and I wouldn't want you to think that I—"

Claire raised a hand. "I wouldn't dream of being upset. I love you, and you love me. You've taken care of me for the better part of your life. I wouldn't be the person I am without you. I'm happy that you're happy. Besides, it will always be the Thomson girls against the world. Now we have a couple of men as our backup, is all."

Granny sent her another wink. "You got that right."

Claire gave her granny a squeeze and then reached her hands out to take the baby from her. Granny relinquished the infant with a slight objection but quickly focused on her new fiancé.

Claire cooed to her daughter and joined Ethan's side. "Can you believe it? We have a new baby and another wedding to plan. So much has happened in such a short time."

Ethan stroked his daughter's cheek and planted a soft kiss on Claire's head. "It has, but I don't regret any of it."

Claire stepped closer, still cuddling Rosemarie. "I don't either." The music swelled, and couples paired up around the room, heading to the dance floor.

Ethan extended a hand toward his bride. "May I have this dance?"

Smiling, Claire turned to her granny. "Do you mind holding your great-granddaughter for a little longer while I dance with my husband?"

Granny grinned and reached for the bundle of joy. "Hand her over. She and I will take a spin around the room to show her off to the guests."

Placing her hand in Ethan's, Claire followed him to the center of the room and allowed him to lead her in a waltz. As they made a path across the floor, Claire's eyes settled on a couple nearby. She gasped.

Michael and Dr. Brickworth remained in a close embrace, swaying to the music, their eyes locked upon one another.

Leaning closer to Ethan's ear, she whispered, "Look over there," and nodded toward the duo.

Ethan glanced in the direction Claire had indicated and chuckled. "It looks like your granny and Nigel aren't the only couple to come out of the Intercontinental Games chaos."

Claire smiled. "I guess not. Should we go over and say something to them?"

Ethan flashed her a wicked grin. "A chance to tease my best friend and offer him best wishes on a new relationship? Absolutely." He twirled Claire several times, inching closer to his best friend. As soon as they were within earshot of the new couple, Ethan tipped his head closer to Michael. "Hey mate, looks like you've found a beautiful dancing partner."

Michael's face flushed crimson, but he looked pleased.

Claire had never seen Ethan's best friend look flustered before. Her thoughts drifted to when Michael helped save the day by showing up with a motorcycle. Typically, he acted cool under pressure. It amused her to see him like this. She grinned. "I didn't realize that you had spent much time together."

Michael stopped swaying, still holding Dr. Brickworth's hands in his. "Well, uh—a"

Dr. Brickworth, dressed in a vibrant red gown that matched her hair, jumped in. "We spent a lot of time together when you both were missing. The two of us were worried, and it helped to have someone to talk to about the whole thing. He shared stories with me about him and Ethan in school and made me laugh." Her eyes darted to Michael, and she blushed.

Ethan tilted his head, and his smile widened.

"Wow, that's wonderful. I had no idea."

Michael shifted his weight. "I'm sorry I didn't get to tell you about this myself. With everything that happened after you two went missing—the emergency with the baby and then the last-minute planning for the Fruhling Gala—I didn't have time to talk to you. But, when I saw this beautiful woman across the room—" His eyes drifted to Dr. Brickworth's face. "I had to ask her to dance."

Ethan released his hold on Claire and waved a dismissive hand. "No worries, mate. I'm thrilled. It's fantastic news. Massive congratulations. I'm glad to see you happy." He reached forward, shook Michael's hand, and gave him a friendly slap on the back.

Michael's face erupted in a huge grin, and the crimson color deepened. "Thanks."

Claire piped in, "Besides, you're not the only couple to come out of the games." She nodded toward the corner of the room where her granny stood holding Rosemarie, Nigel practically glued to her side. "Granny has a new beau, and it's serious."

Michael raised his brow. "Oh, really? How serious?"

"Super serious. They're engaged." She nodded to emphasize the point.

Michael chuckled. "That's amazing news. I've always liked your granny. I just hope that Nigel can keep up with her."

Claire tilted her head and glanced at her granny

once more. The woman who'd helped raise her was now doing the jitterbug with Rosemarie while Nigel attempted to follow along. "I won't say that thought didn't cross my mind. She's a handful, but Nigel has managed my rascally dog, all of the chaos of the snow squall, and my delivery, not to mention last-minute plans for the gala, so if anyone can tame my granny, it's him."

Ethan laughed at this sentiment. "True." He glanced at his best friend again and then winked at Claire. "We should let these two lovebirds have some time alone. Plus, I want to finish my dance with my wife." Turning to Michael, he gave him one last shoulder slap and stepped back. With a grand gesture of presenting his hand to Claire, he lowered his head to a deep bow. "My lady."

She shook her head at her husband's silliness but secretly enjoyed the display of affection. "Ethan's right. We must finish our dance and make our rounds to the other guests." Claire dipped her head toward the pair and then turned to place her hand in Ethan's.

Michael and Dr. Brickworth said their goodbyes and resumed a cozy discussion, their heads close together.

Ethan rose and gathered her other hand in his, drawing her close. He gazed down into her eyes, and his voice thickened, "Thank you for doing me the honor of dancing with the most beautiful woman in the room."

His words sent a shiver down her back, and her

pulse quickened. Claire marveled at the effect her husband still had on her. Ethan's strong arms encircled her, and he swayed her side to side, not bothering with the formalities of the waltz this time. He pulled her closer, his lips close to her ear. "I know how everyone is watching, and we will probably end up on the morning paper causing another scandal, but I don't care."

Claire raised a brow and turned her head, peering into his eyes. "A scandal? Over what? Dancing? My grandmother does prefer we waltz, but I can't see how an American slow dance could cause a riot."

Ethan stopped swaying and stood still. He traced the outline of her cheek with his thumb and then tipped her chin up toward his face. "Not over the dancing. Over this." Then, he lowered his lips and pressed them against hers, melting into her.

Claire closed her eyes, and her heart pounded. Propriety went out the window as she wrapped her arms around Ethan's neck and deepened her kiss. Her heart pounded, her fingertips tingled, and she forgot about time or space. She marveled that her husband still made each kiss feel like the first one—exciting and new.

A few seconds later, Ethan lifted his head and gazed into his wife's eyes. "I love you—more now than ever before. Claire, you are a remarkable woman. You've grown stronger over the past few months and have been brave. The Amorley people are blessed to have you, and I thank God every day that we get to spend our lives together."

Tears stung Claire's eyes. "I love you, too. I'm the blessed one. God gave me a wonderful family and a great group of people to support me on this journey. I couldn't do any of it without you and them. If I've become stronger, it's only because of God's love and yours." Staring into her husband's eyes, Claire murmured, "I—"

Having a knack for interrupting at just the right moment, Granny sidled up next to Claire and Ethan. "You two lovebirds have had enough alone time. This little miss told me she's hungry, and I get the feeling she's like all Thomson women—impatient."

Rosemarie let out a wail that pierced the room as if to confirm this suspicion. Claire waved for her granny to hand over the baby. "Give her to me. She wants her mom." She took the infant in her arms and whispered sweet words into the child's ear, "You are the sweetest girl. Mommy loves you."

Within seconds the baby quieted, and the wailing subsided. Soon she closed her eyes and drifted off to sleep.

Granny snorted. "How do you like that? I guess she's a momma's girl."

Claire grinned. "I guess so."

Nigel joined Granny, and seeing that she'd been released from babysitting duty, he extended a hand to her. "Would you like to dance?"

Granny giggled like a schoolgirl and placed her

hand in his. "I would love that." She glanced at Claire. "You don't mind, do you?"

Claire chuckled, still rocking the baby in her arms. "Not at all. Enjoy the gala. Thank you for looking after Rosemarie for me."

Granny flashed her a wide smile. "Anytime. Rosemarie and I are going to be best friends. Now, I've got a hot date to get back to and a dance floor to light up."

Shaking her head, Claire watched as her vivacious granny sashayed away with her fiancé. Joy filled her heart, and she'd never felt so happy and complete. She turned her gaze to Ethan, and her smile faded upon seeing his frown. "What's wrong?"

Ethan's eyes became serious. "It occurred to me again that I almost lost you and Rosemarie. I don't know what I would've done if something had happened to the two of you. I don't want to spend another moment away from you or her."

Claire smiled. "Neither do I," she agreed as she swayed side to side gently with her daughter and the heir to the Amorley crown. The future looked bright, and gratitude for her blessings overwhelmed her. Her throat tightened, and happy tears filled her eyes. She gazed at her true love, the one who'd captured her heart, and smiled. "Neither do I," she whispered once more.

# Epilogue

Claire paced the hallway outside of the main parliament galley. She could do this. All of the self-doubt and fear she'd carried with her the past year had drifted away, but that didn't completely dissipate her public speaking anxiety.

Ethan appeared in the doorway and sent her an encouraging smile. "Everyone's seated, and the press has arrived. They're ready for you. Are you nervous?"

Halting her attempt to run a pathway into the ground, Claire paused and arched a brow. "Who? Me? Nervous about speaking my mind to a room filled with all the members of parliament and every major press outlet nationwide? Never."

Ethan chuckled and stepped closer to her. He gave her shoulders a squeeze and gazed into her eyes. "You are going to be amazing. Brilliant. Today marks the day my wife changes the course of Amorley history for womankind. I couldn't possibly be prouder." He leaned down and planted a soft kiss on her forehead.

Sending her husband a quick grin, she released a

breath she'd held for several seconds. "Right. Changing history. I'll focus on that and not the memory of one of the last times I spoke before parliament and vomited, publicly announcing my pregnancy in an unprecedented way."

Ethan laughed. "Yes, let's not do that again. Your grandmother is an understanding woman, but I think she can only handle one of those episodes in her lifetime." He gave her another squeeze. "You better go. It's time for you to change Amorley's future."

She nodded and headed out the doorway and up the stairs leading to the stage where she would speak. Approaching the podium, she drew in one last deep breath and exhaled. Taking the gavel that rested on the podium in hand, she banged it three times, and the room fell silent. Claire glanced at the queen mother.

Her royal grandmother shook her head with outward disapproval. She hated seeing anyone other than a parliament member use the gavel, but she sent her granddaughter a slight smile.

Claire grinned. Her grandmother was proud, and she should be. Today marked an important change in Amorley history and proved a breakthrough for future Amorley women.

"Hear ye, hear ye," Claire called to the room. She'd always wanted to say that. Granny snickered from the front row. Scanning the crowd, Claire began, "Today, change has happened because all of you were willing to open your minds and hearts. Just because something has always been done a certain way does not necessarily make it right. In the case of the article in the Amorley Constitution that required its ruler to provide proof of an heir or a pregnancy within the first year of rule to solidify the ruler's leadership, I am happy to say that with a unanimous vote by our Parliament—"

Granny lifted her hand. "—and after a wonderful speech by my granddaughter—"

Claire's face warmed. "Yes, thank you, Granny. I appreciate the kindness of Parliament in listening to my words and making the right decision by voting to change an outdated and archaic rule. It gives me great pleasure to say that moving forward, there will be no requirement for proof of an heir to confirm a ruler's position."

The crowd broke into applause and stood to its feet.

Claire glanced at her husband, who stood behind her, holding her beautiful, blonde daughter. The baby shoved her tiny fist in her mouth and smiled.

As much as happiness filled her heart over the fact that she'd helped make a positive change for her country and her daughter's future, a deeper sense of gratitude overwhelmed her for God's gift of her family. Joyful tears filled her eyes, and Claire grinned.

Her daughter blew her mother a kiss and gave an adorable, baby-fisted wave, which evoked a burst of appreciative oohs and has from the audience.

Claire walked over to join her family and kissed

her daughter on the cheek. "You are the most beautiful, wonderful little girl in the world. No matter what happens in the future, God will take care of us. You don't ever have to be afraid." She lifted her head and gazed into Ethan's eyes. "I love you."

Ethan grinned and swayed with his daughter. "I love you, too," he whispered.

Claire didn't doubt that the future would carry with it trials and tribulations but tucked away in her heart was the deep certainty that God would be with her, and no matter what came her way, she had nothing to fear and everything for which to rejoice. She leaned in close and rested her face against her daughter's cheek. "I love you, too."

## Also by Jill Boyce:

*Harte Broken*

## About the Book:

Time doesn't heal all wounds. Love does.

Amy Harte, an Emergency Medicine physician, lost her mother to cancer suddenly on the day of her residency graduation one year ago. As a doctor, she struggles with not being able to save her mother and experiencing her best day on her worst. Since then, she has turned from her relationship with God in her guilt and grief. Near the fateful day's anniversary, her father calls to tell Amy the bank may take her childhood home. Amy knows she must save the house that holds the last precious memories of her mother.

Meanwhile, Amy meets a gorgeous Christian man, Seth, who slowly restores her belief in love and God's goodness. Their happily ever after may have to wait because Dr. Mark Blakely, Amy's dashing hospital colleague, has never met a woman he couldn't woo. Still, Amy suspects Mark values the chase more than her heart. Time is running out for Amy to save her family home and release her anger and guilt. Will she discover that love, especially God's love, heals all wounds?

## Sneak Peek the First Chapter:

Psalm 147:3 He heals the brokenhearted and binds

up their wounds.

## Chapter 1
July 2, 2017, Sunday

Amy Harte stared at the brass nameplate in front of her as she knelt on the cool green lawn. She ran her fingers over the letters, tracing the precious name. Her gaze shifted to the tilted vase attached to her mother's headstone, and she reached out to straighten it. A light breeze blew past, carrying the sharp scent of freshly cut grass.

"I'm sorry, Mom. I'm so sorry." Only silence answered. She drew in a shuddering breath. Today marked an anniversary she never wanted to celebrate. One year ago, Amy had graduated from residency and fulfilled a lifelong dream to become a physician—but on that same day, she lost her mother. How does one celebrate when the best day of life is also the worst?

Guilt washed over Amy as she reflected on how she'd let her mother down. She'd missed being with her when she passed and still carried the burden of failure to save her mom despite being a physician tasked with healing others.

The phone call Amy had received earlier that morning from her father rose in her thoughts. "Hello," she'd mumbled.

"Amy? Did I wake you?" Her father's low-timbered voice bellowed.

"Dad, are you okay?" Amy rubbed the sleep out of her eyes and tried to gain her bearings.

"Yes," her dad's voice trailed off.

"What's going on?" The last year's events flashed through her mind, and she felt a rock developing in the pit of her stomach.

"It's about the house. I got a call Friday morning from the bank and met with the manager."

Amy ran a hand through her hair, relaxing a bit. "Dad, you haven't had a mortgage in years."

"Well, that's true. We did pay it off a few years ago."

"Okay, so then what's the problem?"

"The problem is that because of the cost of your mom's treatments and then the funeral, I had to take out a second mortgage on the house. I didn't know what else to do…"

She frowned. "So, what does this mean? Can't we ask the bank for an extension? I'm sure they'll understand."

"They understand, but that doesn't change the fact that the bill is due. The bank manager said that I have sixty days to come up with the rest of the loan, $50,232, or the house will go to foreclosure," his voice cracked.

She could tell he was close to tears. "Oh, Dad. Don't cry. We'll figure something out." Amy wracked her brain, calculating her student loan balance, which teetered over the six-figure mark, and considered her rent and car payment. She just started working at Metropolitan Hospital, so her savings account was anemic.

"They can't take your home." She'd had tea parties there with her mother. It was where she had learned to ride a bike and gotten ready for prom. "Where would you live?" Amy tried to conceal the rising panic in her voice.

"Don't worry about me. The money from my pension more than covers my monthly living expenses, and I'm sure I could find something reasonable to rent."

"No. Absolutely not. We lost mom. We can't lose the family home."

"Well, if you come up with a way to make fifty-grand

in the next sixty days, let me know. Otherwise, I think it would be a good idea if you came over in the next few weeks to go through things."

"Don't start packing up yet, Dad. I love you." Amy hung up and made a silent vow to save her childhood home.

A butterfly landed on her hand, snapping Amy out of the memory. Hot tears stung her eyes, and a single droplet rolled down her cheek. She wiped it away and shook her head. No time for tears today. She stood and brushed tiny blades of grass off her faded mint-green scrub pants.

A grey-haired older gentleman dressed in overalls stood a few feet away, raking mulch into a flowerbed. "You've got to receive God's forgiveness sometime, young lady." He continued his work as he spoke, not lifting his head.

Amy stood straighter and pressed her lips into a firm line. "Excuse me, what did you say?"

The stranger halted his task and rested his arm on the rake. His eyes found Amy's. "I said, you're going to have to accept God's forgiveness…only way to move forward. Guilt will eat you up inside and make it hard to love and live." The man shrugged and resumed his work as if never a word was spoken.

Her mouth fell open. *What does he know about God's forgiveness? He's probably crazy.* She started to refute his intrusion, but her pager beeped, reminding her to get moving. She walked to her car and hopped inside.

The muggy summer air, combined with choking grief, made breathing difficult. She cranked up the air conditioning and drove across town, arriving at the parking lot of Scottsburg, Virginia's community hospital. She stopped the car, stamped down the emergency brake, and paused. "Come on, Amy. Get it together. You're a professional." She slid out of the car and walked toward the hospital with hurried steps.

Straightening her shoulders, Amy stepped past the main glass doors of Metropolitan Hospital and entered the five-star, luxury-hotel-like foyer. Despite the crystal chandelier hanging overhead and a white marble floor below, the classic scent of bleach revealed it to be a well-endowed medical facility with an expansive, wealthy board of directors and donors.

Amy strode into the Emergency Department and sent a nod to her best friend and lead respiratory therapist. "Hey Beth, how's it looking today? Swamped already?"

Beth, petite with shoulder-length blond hair, leaned against the central nursing station, the main activity hub. She flicked her hand with a quick wave and grinned. "Hey, Amy!" Glancing at the large whiteboard filled with patients' names and room assignments confirmed her assessment.

Blowing her bangs out of her eyes, Beth nodded her head. "Yeah, it's been a madhouse. I thought people slept in on Sundays."

"I suppose some people use Sundays to get things done. You know… laundry, dishes, late brunches, grocery store runs… or go to church, I guess."

Some people, but not Amy. Tears threatened to spill over again, but she turned her head away and forced them back down. She held her breath. A gentle hand settled on her arm, and Amy met Beth's sympathetic eyes.

"Hey, do you need to go home? I know this must be a hard day for you. If you want, I can tell them you didn't feel well."

She gulped in a fresh breath of air and exhaled. Amy shook her head. "No, I'm fine." As she reached for a chart, the overhead paging system announced an incoming emergency.

An ambulance siren blared, and two EMTs burst through the ED's double doors.

Amy rushed toward them.

The first medic rattled off statistics. "Victim is Brian Broadstone, driver in a two-car motor vehicle accident. He suffered a head trauma and suspected concussion, with a laceration to the right scalp. Vitals are stable."

She shifted her eyes from the patient to the medic. "Thanks, I'll take it from here." She grabbed her stethoscope from her neck and began her exam. After finding the patient in stable condition, she sent him to get a head CT.

The emergency department double doors parted again, and a tall, handsome man with dark brown hair burst through them. His eyes widened as he saw Brian's stretcher roll away.

"Hey, where's my brother going?"

He wore a black short sleeve t-shirt stretched snugly across his broad chest and thick shoulders and flattered his fit physique. His chiseled jaw clenched, and concern clouded his chestnut eyes.

Amy's cheeks warmed, and she blinked hard. *Pay attention.* She shook her head, gathering her thoughts. "Hi, I'm Dr. Amy Harte. Your brother's stable, but I sent him off for imaging. A head injury warrants a thorough workup. Were you in the car with him?" She smiled, hoping to ease his worry.

"Yeah, sorry I'm late. I rode over in the ambulance but stepped outside for a minute to call my dad. I didn't want my parents to hear about the accident from someone else."

Nodding her head, Amy understood. She knew how Scottsburg's rumor mill operated.

The handsome man met Amy's gaze, and his serious expression relaxed as he took a few steps closer. "Is he going to be okay?"

"I think he'll be fine, but I don't want to miss anything. Are you okay? We can evaluate you, too."

"I'm fine. Not a scratch on me." He stretched his hand toward Amy. "I should introduce myself. My name is Seth."

She shook his hand, and a shiver traveled down her spine at his touch. Releasing his grip, she cleared her throat. "Nice to meet you. If your brother's tests are normal, then he may be able to go home tonight as long as someone stays with him." Amy attempted to keep her tone even and professional. "Where were you guys headed so early this morning?"

The good-looking stranger grinned and shifted his weight. "Well, this week is our mother's birthday, so we were headed to grab breakfast, then take in the early church service so we'd have time to get things together afterward for her big day."

She raised her brow. "Did you make it to breakfast?"

Seth shook his head. "No, we didn't. Come to think of it, I'm starving. Do you think I have time to run to the cafeteria and grab something before Brian gets back?"

Amy smiled and nodded. "Sure. That's fine. I'll let him know where you went. If you're like me, it's hard to function before coffee."

Seth nodded. "Same." Seth searched her face, his eyes warm with interest. "Would you like a cup? I'll bring you one back."

Amy's cheeks burned, and her palms grew damp. Her fingertips tingled. She longed to say yes, but she feared that the names on the whiteboard were multiplying by the minute.

Someone tapped her on the shoulder. She turned, and Dr. Mark Blakely stood with two foam cups in hand.

Mark wore a confident grin as he eyed Seth. "No worries. I've got it covered." He passed one of the cups to Amy.

She hesitated, then accepted it. "Thanks, Mark."

Disappointment flashed across Seth's face for a moment. "Okay. Thanks again for taking great care of my brother." He smiled and reached out to shake Amy's hand again. "I'll be right back." Seth turned and walked away.

Mark left Amy's side to attend to another incoming patient.

Amy wished she could have talked to Seth longer, but Mark had impeccable timing.

Mark asked her out on a date weekly, despite her lack of encouragement. She suspected Dr.

Blakely's dating record included most of the female population of Scottsburg.

Amy approached Beth standing at the nursing station and noticed an unmistakable smirk on her best friend's face. "So, I see you've met the new Chief Financial Officer."

Exhaling for the first time in a minute, Amy asked, "What do you mean?"

Beth's grin widened, and she crossed her arms in front of her chest. "Seth Broadstone. The charge nurse told me your patient's brother is the new CFO of the hospital. Apparently, he started a few weeks ago. So, this should be interesting. I saw the look between the two of you."

She winked.

Amy rolled her eyes. "I don't know what you're talking about…there was no look. Besides, right now, I don't have time to date anybody. I have a lot on my mind." Her thoughts drifted to the conversation she'd had with her dad about her parent's house. "I'm channeling all my energy into work." She owed it to her mom.

Beth's face fell, and she grew serious. "Hey, I get it. Your work is your life…but don't forget to make time for some fun, too. I guess we hadn't met Seth yet because he's stationed on the floor with the administrators."

Shrugging in nonchalance, Amy agreed, "You're probably right." She secretly hoped this wouldn't be the last time their paths crossed.

**Author Biography:**

Jill writes inspirational romantic fiction with a medical theme. She is an Amazon best-selling author and the first two novels in her Royal Medicine Series, Royally Confused and Royally Engaged are 2022 Selah Award Finalists. Her work has also won Firebird Book Awards for Harte Broken, Perfectly Imperfect, A Prescription for Beauty, and Royally Confused.

Her debut novels are part of the A Dose of Love series. Each story can stand alone, but each features a strong female lead facing challenging life circumstances while finding love along the way. Jill's first novel, Harte Broken, was inspired by her love of romance and her walk through the grief of losing her mother on the same day of her daughter's birth. It raises the question, "What happens when the best day is also the worst one?"

Jill is a physician turned stay-at-home mom, who loves coffee, travel, and anything glittered. She treasures spending time with her husband and children, who are her heart and greatest joy.

Please join her at www.jillboyceauthor.com to stay updated on upcoming releases and reader news.

**Let's stay in touch! Follow me on:**

Facebook to enjoy #fun, faith, hope…and a little coffee!

Jill Boyce, Author, LLC


Check out my website— www.jillboyceauthor.com to join my monthly newsletter and hear about my puppy's latest hijinks, new releases, discounts, giveaways, and other great deals!

Connect with me on Twitter or Instagram as well!

Join me on Goodreads and BookBub to find out what I'm reading!

# Books By Jill Boyce

A DOSE OF LOVE SERIES

*Harte Broken (Book One)*
*Perfectly Imperfect (Book Two*
*A Prescription for Beauty (Book Three)*


ROYAL MEDICINE SERIES

*Royally Confused (Book One)*
*Royally Engaged (Book Two)*
*Royally Married (Book Three)*
*Royally Blessed (Book Four)*


!